# Echoes in the Glass

**Dolores, Volume 2**

Hayden Thorne

Published by Hayden Thorne, 2018.

ECHOES IN THE GLASS

*

Copyright © 2018 Hayden Thorne
Cover Art © Hayden Thorne

*

# Also by Hayden Thorne

**Arcana Europa**
Guardian Angel
The Flowers of St. Aloysius
Hell-Knights
Children of Hyacinth
The Amaranth Maze
A Murder of Crows

**Curiosities**
Dollhouse
Automata
Eidolon

**Dolores**
Ambrose
Echoes in the Glass
A Dirge for St. Monica

**Ghosts and Tea**
The Ghosts of St. Grimald Priory
Agnes of Haywood Hall

A Most Unearthly Rival
The Haunted Inkwell
The House of Creeping Dolls


**Grotesqueries**
A Castle for Rowena
The Rusted Lily
Primavera


**Masks**
Masks: The Original Trilogy
Curse of Arachnaman
Mimi Attacks!
Dr. Morbid's Castle of Blood
The Porcelain Carnival


**Standalone**
Renfred's Masquerade
Rose and Spindle
Gold in the Clouds
Helleville
Icarus in Flight
Arabesque
Banshee
Wollstone
The Glass Minstrel
Henning
The Twilight Gods
The Book of Lost Princes
The Winter Garden and Other Stories

Desmond and Garrick
The Cecilian Blue-Collar Chronicles

Watch for more at https://haydenthorne.com.

# Table of Contents

# Chapter 1

"Goddamn motherfu—" A string of obscenities poured out of Quinn in a glorious explosion of verbal filth. He stopped jiggling the key, took a step back, and inhaled deeply. Adjusting the loaded grocery bag in his arm, he reached out and knocked on the door. "Grandma! I'm home! Can you open the door? Fucking deadbolt won't turn again!"

A handful of seconds later, he heard the muffled shuffling of feet from inside the house. The familiar sounds of a human-versus-ancient-mechanical-thing struggle followed, and the door swung open on loud hinges. And before him stood his five-foot-tall grandmother, a ferocious scowl in place as she peered up at him.

"I'd like to hex a bar of soap for that sewer mouth of yours, mister," she barked. "Don't you think I didn't hear what you said. My body might be rotting away in old age, but my hearing's as sharp as ever. And you had the gall to overcompensate for that filthy muttering by yelling cuss words for all the world to hear just because the lock wouldn't turn."

She moved away and busied herself with Quinn's key while Quinn stooped to pick up the second bag of groceries. Without handles on them, it required an acrobat's skill to pick it up, secure it against his chest (both with just one hand and its corresponding long-suffering arm), and stand up again without staggering or dropping anything. *And* without losing his glasses, which had a bad habit of sliding off his face at the most inconvenient moment because he just *had* to get a pair of somewhat oversized hipster frames. But Quinn was used to it, and it almost felt like awkward ballet whenever he managed things successfully. He entered the house, his irritation easing at least.

"Grandma, all bad habits I have, I got from you. Stop being so salty. And since you're not a sorcerer, you can quit the hex threats."

"I'm a thread alchemist, kid, and don't you sass me like that." She eyed the bags in shock as though she'd just noticed them for the first time. "What the fu—hell? I thought you were going out to get us a 'few things.'"

Quinn sighed as he stalked past the narrow stairs and through the small-ish living room toward the dining room door. "You're a hardcore cross-stitch hobbyist, and you're changing the subject."

He eventually reached the dining table and gladly set the bags on it with a loud groan of relief. Quinn Geiger might only be twenty-one, but even a healthy young man had his physical limits. Then again, he chided himself, he'd also decided to throw in a few items not on his grandmother's grocery list—items he simply couldn't do without like a couple of one-pound bags of gummy bears, among others—so he really shouldn't be so bitchy about things. And given the way his morning had turned out, those bags would definitely come in handy.

With an inward sigh, Quinn tried not to think too much about his disastrous not-date at the café.

"A hardcore cross-stitch hobbyist who puts out some crazy, badass patterns that don't end," Grandma barked as she shuffled into the room behind him. "And all coming from the spirit world, too. There. Have you ever heard of other cross-stitch artists or hobbyists who can brag about that kind of stuff? No? Then I win. God, don't tell me you splurged on bags of candy again."

"Didn't realize sewing bizarre patterns was a competition," Quinn muttered. He was now putting groceries away and mentally groaning at his grandmother's never-ending, cranky prattle.

"At my age, mister, I can call anything whatever I damn well like. Been fighting through the toxic waves of life like diseased salmon, so I earned the right. Have you been losing weight again? What the hell's wrong with your metabolism?"

Quinn glanced at her with a crooked smile. "You should've been a poet. Did you just hear yourself? I'll bet you'd rock an open mic night at some hipster café."

Grandma snorted and moved to the table to give Quinn a hand. "Those are your paternal genes expressing themselves again. Christ, kid. And here I thought your father holed up somewhere in Japan spared me extra years of grief. Looks like I forgot the whole popping-out-the-grandkid issue."

"And who gave birth to Dad and cursed him with snarky genes, Grandma?"

"He's a changeling, I'll bet. Somewhere in fairy land, there's a perfectly normal human man trapped there and thinking he's one of those creepy magic whatsits. And speaking of—how'd your coffee date go?"

Quinn didn't know how much more of Grandma's whiplash-style shifts in topic his brain could handle without exploding in its barely-held-together bony container. He also wasn't too enthused about the subject she now decided to highlight, too, and he hated lying to her.

So he did.

"It went okay. Matt and I didn't really hit it off as much as I'd like to, though. But, you know, que sera sera and all that stuff," he replied with a careless shrug as he pointedly avoided looking at her.

Grandma sighed heavily. "Oh, honey. The bastard stood you up, didn't he? Just like the others?"

"It's—it's okay, Grandma. Really. It's not the end of the world."

"What the hell's wrong with young people nowadays? If they don't want to show up for a date they made, how about—oh, I don't know—letting the other person know it's off? Why leave him hanging and looking stupid and feeling like shit about himself?" Grandma damn near roared. "You know what, baby? Screw them! They're nothing but a bunch of immature douchebags who can't man up to—"

"Grandma, it's cool. It's cool. I'll survive. Been there, done that. I think of that as character-building, sort of."

This time Quinn glanced back and met her furious gaze with a smile that he hoped exuded confidence and reassurance. He felt neither, of course, but he wasn't in the mood to put up with his grandmother's tirades, even if they were spewed on his account. Being stood up by other young men—more than half of whom, ironically, were the ones who'd asked him out—was nothing new to Quinn. He didn't understand why he was such a magnet for that kind of behavior or why he somehow unknowingly gravitated toward the handsome and the immature. Was he inadvertently punishing himself for something? Did he dislike himself enough to give off low self-esteem vibes that others picked up and were influenced by so that their subsequent mistreatment of him was the unhappy consequence?

"You might think it's character-building, but I hate it. I do. You're my grandson, and I want to see you happy."

"I know. I love you, too." Quinn turned his attention back to his task. "I have to finish this. I don't have much time left."

Grandma suddenly fell silent, and when the pause stretched to rather unnatural lengths, Quinn had to look back over his shoulder, frowning. He found her standing still, wrinkled face fixed in an expression of hard concentration, her mind clearly chasing after some idea she was bound to share.

"Grandma? What's wrong? You're creepily quiet." Quinn turned back and finished shelving the cans of sweet corn and closing the cupboard doors.

"Huh. Nothing. Just thinking about your father now. I kind of miss the globetrotting jerk." She blinked, looked up, and regarded Quinn doubtfully at first and then broke out in a big, silly grin. Obviously the cause of her rage had already been forgotten, making Quinn wonder if old age did funny things to the turn of one's mind—besides senility, that is. "And Bethany said hi. She said you eat too many gummy bears, and your habit's going to give you diabetes."

Quinn rolled his eyes and finished unpacking the bags, shooing her away a couple of times when she got a little too pushy in her bid to help him. "That's not how diabetes works, you know. And tell Bethany to lay off. I've got enough trouble sorting you out. I don't need an imaginary friend riding my ass over a candy habit."

"Well, she does get worried about you."

"She doesn't exist. And imaginary friends are normally a childhood thing. Don't tell me you're a late bloomer."

Grandma actually had to pause and consider that, screwing up her face and keeping it contorted long enough for Quinn to wonder if she were severely impacted and hadn't been up front with her one and only grandson about her health. At length she eased up.

"Nope, not a late bloomer. Bethany's around—been around for a while, she tells me. And the patterns I sew are not only badass, but unique." Grandma let a dramatic pause run its course. "Because she's showing me what her world looks like."

"Okay, Grandma. Time to lay off the hard stuff, okay? Seriously. I'm going to have to search your room for hiding places and shit," Quinn retorted, more annoyed than worried.

This was a conversation that was too common, going on for a good number of months now ever since Quinn moved back home. That said, these talks about imaginary friends didn't happen as frequently till now.

Grandma merely chortled, and she spun around and hobbled back out, no doubt to take her place again in her favorite "hobby room", which was also her little bedroom on the ground floor. She was simply too old to get up and down the stairs without trouble, and it was Quinn's desperate idea to have her things moved to the tiny room that had once been a study of some sort. The second flight of stairs led to the attic, which had been converted into Quinn's bedroom on his move back home from college. He could, of course, take over his grand-mother's massive old room, but he loved his attic bedroom and reveled in its gothic, antiquated look and atmosphere. It suited him perfectly, he thought, given his job: the assistant manager of a small, independent bookstore special-izing in all manner of darkly fantastic books.

Besides, Grandma's old room smelled too much like pain relief ointment and talcum powder.

His mind flew back through time, touching events here and there till the moment he'd decided to pack his bags and return home. He didn't even know why he'd felt so strongly then, felt the sudden and overwhelming need to hop on the train and come back to Dolores even before he finished college. A voice-less urging seemed to be the closest description he could think of at that time, and now that he'd spent a year in his grandmother's company, he wondered if that had been his mother's long-silent voice calling for him to return home and look after the old woman.

Grandma had always been rather salty, but she was also fiercely protective of and devoted to her only grandson as well as Quinn's parents despite her oc-casional insults, which Quinn had long learned were nothing more than a sin-gular way of expressing immeasurable love. She'd also developed an unexpected late talent for cross-stitching bizarre patterns, claiming she'd been getting them from the spirit world. And bizarre they were, indeed—strange figures, shapes, and even what seemed to be landscapes or vague details of landscapes slowly and painstakingly took shape in her skilled hands. And it wasn't several unus-able pillow covers she'd been working on.

Like Penelope of legend, Grandma had been sewing what appeared to be a never-ending tapestry of some sort. She'd already gone through so many skeins of embroidery floss, very likely her monthly social security checks all but disap-pearing thusly. But not once had she complained of either the time spent or her arthritis. She loved being kept busy, in fact, even claiming that she often talked to Bethany while working in her room or the living room.

Bethany, of course, was her imaginary friend, one whom Grandma was con-vinced used to be a living, breathing woman sometime in the past. And sometimes she'd dive into a lengthy account of Bethany's so-called world, which was apparently a dark and terrifying one if the patterns in her cross-stitched tapestry were anything to go by. Quinn had always treated her idiosyncrasies as nothing more than a natural effect of age, and even her doctor had given her a clean bill of health. But now and then, her glib references to a world neither of them could see unnerved Quinn, and it was all he could do to allow her imagination its wild flights if they offered her some comfort and distraction. He was young; he could endure the eerie little bits Grandma deigned to share with him.

He sighed heavily and finally cleared the room, making sure the paper bags were properly disposed in the recycling bin. He was set to close the bookstore that evening, so he needed to head upstairs and take a shower before warming up leftovers for lunch. As he walked past the living room and ascended the narrow stairs, he passed a small mirror hanging on the wall and barely gave it a half-second glance.

He froze on the step, frowning. "Wait, what?"

He turned and looked at the mirror again but found nothing unusual about it. Just his reflection and those of the living room windows across the way. There was no one else there, which, for some reason, his brain convinced him had been the case a scant second or two ago. No, there was no one there in the mirror, meeting his brief gaze with one of their own. Was it a figure? Yes, Quinn thought he'd just glimpsed another person moving the other way—down the stairs, that is—and that person turned to look at the mirror at the same moment he did.

All that was impossible, naturally, and Quinn shook his head at himself.

There was, however, one thing that left a strong enough impression—largely because it lingered, and it made him shrink instinctively away, skin prickling. He apparently stood in a spot of icy air, one directly before the mirror. It lingered, yes, but seemed to do so as a way of insisting that Quinn took notice of its presence. And once he did, it went away almost instantly and left Quinn standing and blinking in some confusion, gazing around him. He even looked up to see if he could somehow find a means through which cold air could enter his home and wasn't surprised to find nothing. No hidden vents, no cracks.

"The weird genes are making themselves known in me now, Grandma," he muttered. "Thanks for nothing."

He turned and continued his walk up the stairs and to his attic room, hoping to hell his day would turn out to be a good one at work.

# Chapter 2

"It's like the freakin' Bayeux Tapestry, I swear to God."

"That's dumb. That thing's long. Like—over two hundred feet or something like that?"

Quinn threw Edwin a long-suffering look. "I'm not kidding. She sews yard after yard of Aida fabric together so that we're looking at—I don't know—this long-ass runner type of thing that she's practically filling up with some pretty weird designs. I mean, she cuts the fabric in half and then sews them together, end to end."

"Aida fabric?" Edwin's close-lipped smile was nowhere near sympathetic.

The shop bell rang, and a trio of teenage goth girls swept inside, barely sparing the two a glance. They immediately scattered midway through the bookstore, and Quinn couldn't help but gape at the way their black-draped figures almost immediately melted into the dimly lit environment. If it weren't for the sound of their movements, one could mistake them for oddly flitting shadows unattached to anything corporeal.

Quinn went back to glaring rather weakly at his boss.

"She's sent me out a hundred million billion times to the fabric store for stuff to use, okay? I know way too much about embroidery now, and I don't even know the first thing about sewing. Like—basic sewing to patch up tears and all that. You know, day-to-day survival crap." Quinn sighed and dug around one of the shelves under the counter and pulled out his bag of gummy bears. It already had been opened, and he snatched two pieces and popped them into his mouth. They did little in raising his mood this time, which worried him into questioning whether or not he was developing a tolerance for his favorite candy.

"It's funny how you eat two of those things at a time. I've seen guys take handfuls and shovel them in their mouths like starving Neanderthals. You? Seriously economical. Not to mention pretty goddamned dainty." Edwin paused and considered, frowning as he regarded Quinn in silence. "Is this a gay thing, man?"

"No, it isn't. I just like to portion out my snacks like this—you know, make them last the whole day if I could. Money doesn't grow on trees in case you haven't noticed. And this is the only vice I have, so deal with it." And to underscore that point further, Quinn plucked a couple more pieces from the bag and made a big show of tossing them unerringly into his mouth.

"I hope that's not all you're having for dinner. I've got a lunch container packed with *lumpia*. Tess told me to make sure and share half of it with you since you're, like, shrinking or something."

Tess was Edwin's wife of ten months, another long-suffering soul caught in the never-ending whirlpool spinning around Edwin Aguinaldo's existence. Both were third-generation immigrants from the Philippines whose love of traditional cuisine came with the overriding need (Edwin would refer to it as a genetic quirk of Filipinos) to feed everyone who ventured within a fifty-mile radius of them.

The pair were also pretty successful entrepreneurs even before marriage, owning and running a dark fantasy store and a bakery specializing in Filipino cakes and pastries. Their respective shops might be small and staffed with maybe one (like in Edwin's case) or no more than three (in Tess's), but they flourished nicely enough in their narrow niches.

"I'll have some, thanks." Quinn turned his attention back to the three goth girls, who were now lost in examination of the shelves. He idly drummed his fingers on the counter as his thoughts wandered down another path. "You know, with all that sewing and talk about this Bethany girl, do you think my grandma's showing symptoms of Alzheimer's? I mean—I never even considered it till now, and it's really freaking me out. Is suddenly developing some mad sewing skills a sign of the disease?"

One of the girls floated past the counter on her way to a locked display cabinet filled with death-themed dolls and elaborately sculpted ghouls. "The internet's your friend, dude," she said in a low, gravelly voice. "Look it up."

Edwin moved away from the counter and toward the corner of the small space allocated to the staff. There sat the old desktop computer, the file drawers, and a computer chair that appeared to be headed for the landfill in a matter of days. That tiny corner was technically Edwin's office, the human resources department, and corporate headquarters. At the other end of the narrow, rectangular space behind the counter was a small café-style table and a matching chair, indicating the staff break room. Thankfully the shop had its own bathroom, and at least it wasn't a mere hole dug into the floor somewhere in that same area. Situated in the back—more specifically outside the back door and accessible only through the dingy alley—it was the shop's pride and joy, hence its unavailability to patrons and protected from unwanted use with the magic of a key.

"Want me to look up the symptoms for you? I might as well—not just for your benefit. Tess's grandfather's going all weird on us, too."

Unless there was something in the water, Quinn suspected his grandmother's bizarre turns to be nothing more than an unfortunate product of age. Of course, it didn't mean he could stop worrying about her.

"Nah. That's okay," he replied. "I might be getting myself all worked up over nothing."

Two of the goth girls walked up to the counter with a few books and graphic novels to purchase, allowing Quinn a much-needed distraction from his thoughts. Eventually the trio left the shop, and silence once again reigned.

"So—what kinds of patterns does your grandmother sew, exactly?" Edwin asked.

Quinn jumped when an open plastic tub suddenly appeared before him, and the familiar smell of deep-fried *lumpia* tickled his nostrils. He gratefully plucked a greasy piece out and took a bite, munching on the now-cold and soggy spring roll as he considered his answer.

"Just—really creepy shit," he replied after swallowing. "Like old, dead trees that look really twisted and almost human-like. Then there are things sticking out of the ground—something like broken parts of old fences or stone monuments. Pieces of stone monuments, I mean. Think of cemeteries and those statues of angels and stuff? Yeah, something like those, but in pieces or they're missing a lot of pieces so that you have to kind of think hard about what they're supposed to look like originally. Vines—lots of them. They're usually hanging off branches or whatever's outside your line of vision, if you know what I mean. Some fog also plus shapes in the fog—human-like shapes, anyway."

Edwin didn't answer right away, though he continued to hold the food container in front of Quinn, who helped himself to another cold and soggy spring roll.

"Your grandma sounds like she's into some pretty hard stuff."

"Yeah, I pretty much said the same thing, and she just about cussed me out."

"Dude, she cusses the whole world out. I've been on the receiving end, my-self, in case you forgot."

"I know, but this was more like a targeted cuss—thing. You know what I mean. Don't make me analyze stuff when I'm trying to have kinda-sorta lunch. It's not good for my brain, especially if blood-sugar levels are still pretty low."

Edwin just quietly chortled. "And it's something she's been doing non-stop now?"

Quinn nodded, half of a *lumpia* in his mouth. "It started somewhere around the time I returned from school. Almost a year ago—maybe nine or ten months ago? Yeah, sometime around there."

"Hmm. Same with her imaginary friend?"

"Yep. She doesn't talk about Bethany a lot, though. Once in a while, sure, but it's still enough to ring all kinds of warning bells in my head. I mean—who talks about some invisible person as though they're actually alive?"

Quinn blew out a breath, spirits dipping a little at reminders of some pretty dire possibilities involving his grandmother's mental health. He dropped his gaze to the counter, barely noting how greasy his fingers had become simply from handling two pieces of Tess's cooking.

"Grandma says that Bethany talks about her world, and what Grandma ends up sewing are things that represent Bethany's world or something like that. Now and then, Bethany tries to communicate with me, too. Like she tells Grandma that I eat too many gummy bears and that I'll end up with diabetes and so on. A few times before she complimented me on my looks and my per-sonality."

Quinn grimaced and shuddered at the memory. He'd have dismissed those compliments as nothing more than Grandma's way of praising him in a more indirect and playful way, but there was always a strange light in her eyes when-ever she "forwarded" Bethany's message. Quinn had never quite figured out how to describe it other than a quiet and emphatic earnestness, one that seemed to border on desperate. As though Bethany, had she actually existed, was overly keen on ensuring he got the message and took it to heart. As to the possible purpose of such a message, he couldn't even begin to guess.

Make him feel better about himself despite his bad luck at finding love, maybe? It sounded like something grumpy grandmothers were more likely to do, not imaginary friends with a fetish for horror movie settings.

"Maybe there's something in the air affecting your grandma. I mean—something sort of coming from the rotting shell next door to you guys. Don't you live in a duplex?"

"Yeah. My family never used to, anyway. But my mom moved us there when Dad started flying overseas for business trips and stuff. I guess the price was cheap since the house next door was practically falling apart. And it's also small enough for three of us with only one big bedroom upstairs and a converted attic above that. Before Grandma came to live with us, anyway, I used the attic room, and Mom and Dad had the main bedroom."

"How can a house have one bedroom?"

"I think there used to be two small ones, and whoever lived in it a while ago decided to tear down the wall and turn everything into one big bedroom. Maybe it was a couple who didn't have kids or something. Don't really know shit about our house's history."

Quinn's mother collapsed and died from an undiagnosed heart condition when he was in grade school. Grandma swooped in from out of state to look after her grandson almost immediately, what with Quinn's father still traveling practically non-stop, though he'd taken one year off from that in order to stay with Quinn as well.

Edwin made a face. "Wonder why that other house was never torn down or even fixed up. If the owner was trying to sell a duplex, they could at least get rid of an eyesore. I'm sure it's hell on your home's value."

Quinn shrugged. "Don't know. From what I understand, no one wanted to touch it."

"Oh—too much work to bother with it or something?"

"No. Nobody wanted to touch it. If you ask Grandma, she'll tell you the second half of the duplex doesn't want to be touched." Quinn considered further, brows furrowing. "If anything, it was actually Mom who hinted at something like that. She used to joke around about being psychic and all that, but no one really took her seriously because—well, duh—she always laughed about it."

The memory gave him pause, however, as he thought long and hard about his mother's curious little turns back in the day. He'd been too young to be sure of things, what with faulty human memory and all that, plus his childhood years were quite golden in his mind's eye. Things he remembered might easily be tainted by a child's rosy view of the world, especially since his early years had been idyllic and full of love. But he did recall his mother dropping a word or two about sensing something or someone no one else could, even staring contemplatively at a specific part of a given room or the stairs. But just as quickly, she shrugged things off and moved on, talking and behaving as though nothing odd had just happened. And not once did she even indulge in a rambling theory or two about her experiences, always treating her so-called abilities like a joke. She used to laugh at herself a lot.

A momentary pause followed. "Okay, yeah, that's pretty goddamn creepy," Edwin said. "Maybe you should do some kind of research on the house. Like, the duplex itself. You know, find out the history and all that and why half of it's completely falling apart." He considered his next question with a very professorial frown. "Your grandma didn't notice anything weird at all about the creepy-house-next-door situation? No scary vibes coming from it? No shadows or freaky-ass voices coming from the walls?"

Quinn could only stare at him with his eyes narrowed. "You've been binge-watching ghost hunting shows again, haven't you? And the answer's no."

"Well, no—until now, anyway. Maybe you should ask her if this Bethany chick is communicating to her from next door or something."

Quinn merely rolled his eyes at Edwin and snagged himself another spring roll to munch on. No, he wouldn't even dare encourage his grandmother to talk more about Bethany and the possibility of the decrepit shell of a house next door possibly being haunted. He had enough on his plate as far as he was concerned. A quiet and more insidious voice in his head argued, however, that he simply didn't want to know the truth.

# Chapter 3

A quick and technically refreshing end-of-the-day shower fell far short of its purpose that evening, and Quinn sighed heavily as he stared at himself in the mirror. He looked awfully pale and haggard, though he could attribute that to his mindless overindulgence in cold and soggy *lumpia*. It was a bad habit of his, really, to greedily devour whatever Edwin offered him in a show of friendship and camaraderie. And because Tess told him to *or else*.

Of course, his mood all day had been spiraling in every direction albeit still aiming for a decidedly southbound end because of his newest dating failure. Who got stood up for a coffee date, for the love of the gods and saints, he asked himself? Who? He seemed to be the only one to suffer along those lines, shame compounding the confusion whenever he wondered about it.

A simple coffee date. Taking place in the morning. At a small but rather pricey café easily accessible to foot traffic.

Yet there he was, sitting at a table as agreed on, waiting and staring wistfully at the door whenever a customer appeared and feeling himself sink lower and lower into the floor when five minutes of waiting turned into ten and then fifteen and twenty. All in all, Quinn had waited a good forty-five minutes for his date, and he wasn't sure how much time people normally gave others when tardiness became an issue.

Matt worked at a high end clothing store in downtown Dolores, and that was where they'd met, with Quinn looking in dismay at the sweaters he wanted to buy and realizing the price was close to a month's worth of his salary. Matt had been courteous and even sympathetic, striking up a conversation out of nowhere with a tongue-tied and bug-eyed Quinn and asking him out for a date. Quinn had been reluctant, knowing too well Matt could do much better than settle for someone like him. But Matt had been insistent, had managed to break through Quinn's defensive barriers, and successfully squeezed a "yes" from him.

They'd exchanged numbers as well, with Quinn self-consciously ringing Matt for a confirmation later that day and receiving one. He didn't think much about the fact that Matt sure sounded amused as hell at being phoned, snickering the whole time they spoke. Quinn thought he caught another voice whispering in the background during their conversation, and he apologized for bothering Matt's evening with the call.

He never admitted to his grandmother earlier that he'd tried to call Matt at the café after thirty minutes of waiting and found his calls blocked. The high end clothing store was now another place to add to Quinn's growing list of places to avoid following a wretched experience at being dumped so unceremoniously. Quinn had been so mortified, he didn't breathe a word of the date to Edwin, who was his one and only best friend and confidant and who would have helped him sort through his questions and his hurt. No—as far as he was concerned, even close friendship had a limit insofar as deep personal injuries were concerned, and he was simply too ashamed of himself to confide in Edwin.

There had to be a line somewhere, he thought. He needed to stop putting himself through these experiences and stop wagging his bony tail whenever a handsome stranger deigned to toss him a scrap of attention. He shook his head at himself in resignation and walked out of the second floor bathroom, flicking the light off along the way.

"You in bed yet, kiddo?"

"Oh, jeez…" Quinn hurried to the balustrade and leaned over. "Grandma! Be quiet! And, no, I just got out of the shower, but I'm on my way up now!"

From somewhere downstairs—very likely the living room, where Grandma spent some of her late night sewing time because it was closer to the kitchen, the refrigerator, and the tiny first floor bathroom—a very unladylike snort came.

"What's the big deal if I yelled? There's no one next door to us! You worried I'd wake up the impatiens outside and they'd get pissed off enough to stop blooming? Don't tell me you're taking a flower species' name literally! We raised you better than that!"

"Wow. You're extra salty this evening. What's up?" Quinn demanded, scowling, though his voice softened a tad. Reminders of his conversation with Edwin regarding his grandmother's possible dementia came back with a vengeance, and guilt and genuine worry now edged his fatigue.

Grandma guffawed. "Nothing's wrong. Just wanted to know if you're in bed already. You had a long day today, and you need your beauty sleep. Go on now. Shoo. Go to bed."

Quinn's scowl eased into a narrow-eyed glare at the stairs. He could see neither hide nor hair of his grandmother, of course, so she was spared his stinging look.

"Okay," he said after a couple of seconds fumbling around for something caustic to say and failing spectacularly at it. It was far too late in the day to go head-to-head in a battle of sarcastic wits, he decided. "I'm going. Good night, Grandma."

"Good night, kiddo. Sleep tight!"

Quinn proceeded upstairs, suspicion and doubt compounding as he thought more and more about Grandma's sudden and altogether not-very-subtle move to shoo him up to his attic room. It was an overly eager move, at that, even laced with a generous helping of awkward sweetness and grandmotherly concern for his welfare. He'd experienced how she was when she expressed or demonstrated serious and sincere worry on his account. This one was—it was different, was all Quinn could dredge up. What on earth was that all about?

He paused once he stepped across the threshold of his room and closed the door behind him.

Late night sewing orgy. Unnaturally solicitous question about bedtime. Extra points for a reference to a long, hard day.

Quinn sighed heavily and rubbed the back of his neck, his gaze fixing itself on the ceiling. "Bethany? If you do exist, I'd really appreciate it if you stopped feeding Grandma all kinds of crazy ideas. It's pretty mean and kind of borderline unnecessary considering how old she is, know what I'm saying? I still have to figure out if she's coming down with Alzheimer's or something, and if you're a ghost who's messing with her head, you're not helping. I'm already not looking forward to figuring out what symptoms are real and what aren't."

Unsurprisingly, Bethany didn't respond—if she did exist as a supernatural component of Quinn's home—which only made things a little worse for Quinn. Now feeling sheepish and stupid at talking to no one, he stalked over to his bed and plopped down on it, moving his head and shoulders and listening to overworked joints crack. Relief washed over him at the loosening of strained body parts, and he bent down to pull his "house socks" off his feet.

"What the..."

Quinn sat up, one hand limply clutching a sock, and he glanced to his right, eyes wide and searching. He wasn't wearing his glasses, but even then, he could still see decently enough without them and without needing to squint or strain his eyes.

Was it a shadow that moved just a second or two ago? Or was it nothing more than a trick of his tired mind? The attic room was well-lit even with only a single bedside lamp providing the necessary illumination. Quinn had never once felt unnerved by anything whenever he lay in bed at night, reading a book. Even when he lay in the dark, staring thoughtfully at the ceiling and wondering when he'd ever get lucky in love, money, or plain life in general, not once was he uneasy at anything. A sudden sound, the hint of a deeper shadow in the darkness, a draft of air coming from some indeterminate point—he'd experienced those a few times over since his childhood, but none of them left him rattled.

It was an old house, it was doomed to get even older than that, and it was half of what had been a duplex once upon a time. When considered altogether, such details might spark something in an overactive imagination, but they'd been an inextricable part of Quinn's early years. Now at twenty-one, he'd reached the pinnacle of youthful cynicism's "been there, done that" mentality.

And yet there was something a little different in that split-second experience, and he couldn't quite put a finger on it.

At length Quinn had to shrug and finish tugging his remaining sock off and tossed it to the floor. He was about to scoot up the bed, his mind fixed on that night's bedtime reading, when he yelped and scooted in the wrong direction. Air met his backside, and he tumbled off his bed with a loud and rather graceless thud.

Once the cloud of shock and confusion cleared, he blinked and stared, bug-eyed, at the mirror standing just a few feet from his bed.

Instead of reflected images of his room, the mirror showed a different scene altogether. Quinn gaped at it in stunned silence, unable to move from where he sat and barely even registering the discomfort of a wood floor's hard impact against a person's buttocks.

"What the hell..." he breathed. "What's happening?"

He waited for a moment, refusing to look away or move a single muscle, but nothing else happened in the mirror. The scene remained the same, however-er, and once Quinn managed to gather his wits, he gingerly shifted and crawled across the floor toward the mirror. It had to be hexed, he thought. It had to be. How else could something so insanely wild and impossible be—well—possible? The room revealed by the mirror didn't seem to be an illusion. He detected no signs of a skilled artist's rendering of a room that could only be described as something out of a surreal fairy tale. And he might be unlearned in the art of magic to recognize signs of supernatural manipulation or whatever sorcerers called the purposeful tweaking of a poor laymen's head for the hell of it.

He was soon near enough to dare a light touch against the mirror's surface. And it was a hard and cold one, forcing him to snatch his hand away with a startled little gasp. Up close like this, he was able to take careful note of the strange room inside the mirror's world.

Magical would be an understatement, he thought. The room, horrifyingly enough, seemed to be the mirror-image—no pun intended—of his. Even in a state of dazed shock, Quinn could still easily make out architectural details and even...

"And even the damn furniture," he whispered, dismayed. "What the ever-loving fuck?"

He could see part of a bed, located exactly where Quinn's bed stood. Even the mirror and the freestanding wardrobe across the room was set exactly where Quinn's were. There were, however, obvious and unnerving differences between the mirror's world and his own.

The furniture was quite dated—Quinn hazarded a guess of perhaps no later than the early 19th century, if his memory of all of those Jane Austen adaptations were accurate. However, there appeared to be vines everywhere, creeping along surfaces, crisscrossing across a wall, even coiling around furniture but not completely enveloping anything. The floor was also laced with vines, though that part of the room seemed to be spared a jungle-like appearance.

Quinn raked a hand through his hair and squinted.

No, the vines were everywhere, but they didn't completely cover anything. If he were to try to put the bizarre scene into words, he'd describe the vines as being meticulously and thoughtfully laid out. There had to be some kind of intelligent influence behind it, not just the usual result of Nature left to her own devices. The vines and the antiquated furnishings gave off a very artistic sort of vibe to Quinn. On further inspection, he saw some clear weathering and decay on the wall and the floor, a few jagged cracks mixing it up with the vines.

An odd golden light brightened up the room though up to a point. There didn't seem to be a specific source anywhere, which made Quinn wonder if the light was coming from everything in the room: every component that made it what it was, including the furnishings. Wood, leaf, fabric, glass—perhaps a magical room like that would have its own rules of physics, and illumination could defy the natural world in Quinn's universe just as much as the strange room's very existence and appearance defied everything else.

"How did this happen?"

Was there something hidden behind the mirror? Quinn doubted it, seeing as how he'd been living with this thing for his entire life, and not once had he noticed anything out of place about it. All the same, he crawled off to the side and peered behind the mirror, blinking again at the obvious absence of hidden cameras, hexed illustrations on the back of the mirror, sigils, or anything remotely logical that could explain the phenomenon he was currently experiencing.

He went back to sit before the mirror, his earlier shock and confusion finally giving way to cautious curiosity. He reached out to press his hand against the mirror's surface again, shivering at the touch of hard, cold glass against his palm. This time around, though, he could have sworn the mirror felt even colder than before—like touching ice, even. When he pulled his hand away, Quinn sighed and suddenly felt exhaustion sweep over him, and he was forced to concede. The peculiar room in the mirror wouldn't be there in the morning, he knew, but he also would rather eat his own balls than stay up all night, watching a mirror.

# Chapter 4

The displaced foghorn startling Quinn out of his morning stupor alerted him to a sofa-crashing grandmother, who'd apparently spent the entire night in the living room, sewing away. With a heavy sigh, he knuckled the remaining haze from his eyes and half-stumbled down the rest of the stairs.

"Grandma?" he croaked, blinking. A few choice words of grandsonly lecturing were poised on his lips, but he ended up swallowing his mini-sermon.

Grandma lay stretched on the sofa, her tiny form cushioned by a throw pillow and buried under her monstrosity of a sewing project. Judging from the loud, bone-rattling snores coming from her, she was quite content where she was, utterly lost in sleep and possibly dreaming about new ways of shaving Quinn's life expectancy by another decade. Quinn shook his head, a little fond smile forming as he picked his way through the insane length of fabric lying in a crumpled and tangled stream on the floor. At least Grandma took care to keep her project as close to her as possible and not let the never-ending tapestry carpet the entire living room floor.

Quinn bent down and kissed her forehead, his eyes straying to the most recent section she'd been working on, and there they stopped. He frowned and gently picked up the fabric, keeping the needle from slipping out of the short length of thread that secured it to an unfinished pattern.

The small section Grandma had recently worked on was a crudely embroidered rendering of two people peering into one shared window—or what appeared to be a window—from opposite sides. Was one a reflection of the other? Or were the two figures representative of something, a deeply significant symbol of some sort, that Grandma had thought fit to include in her strange, rambling tapestry? Another detail about the pair of figures and the shared window was the fact that, hovering just behind each of them was a nearly shapeless form, though certain details about the two curious forms indicated females. Or at least the impression Quinn got was that of two barely realized female forms. There were a few differences between the two, however, though perhaps Quinn shouldn't take those details for granted.

One female figure appeared to be smaller and closer in general shape to, well, ordinary women in Quinn's world. The other female figure was larger, looked more grotesque and monstrous, even lacking human-like qualities despite the overwhelming feeling of it being another woman. The second figure, moreover, stood behind the smaller form that peered through the window with a distinct air of threat about it. It loomed over the form, appearing as though it were arching over it in a protective sort of attitude. Like a large and misshapen wave, almost, with the minor indication of arms raised at its sides as though it were blocking the view from the other side.

Quinn scowled as he considered. Was it protecting the smaller figure against the other two?

He turned his attention to the other two figures and compared the female shape, blinking in some surprise at the feeling—one that was faint yet insistent—that the smaller woman was also protecting someone or something. The figure positioned before her, perhaps? Logic would say yes to that, but somehow Quinn had doubts, and he'd no idea why he felt that way. He simply had nothing concrete to base his beliefs on, yet his response to his grandmother's patterns was startlingly visceral and unwavering.

Around the four figures, random details of the environment were sewn—apparently hastily, at that. Tree-like branches or probably vines surrounded one pair, and only what looked to be a lamp and a small table provided the backdrop for the other pair.

Quinn had never really given his grandmother's work a close perusal like this. In the past, he'd always been quick and even dismissive about it, at times his concern for her possible mental health issues making it difficult for him to take the time and look. Really look. She'd never said a thing about it—not a word of complaint for his lack of interest, not a joking insult about his skewed priorities. She'd merely laughed or rolled her eyes before losing herself back in her work, an air of absolute pleasure wrapped around her.

Now that he was there, startled out of his own selfishness by the new patterns she'd sewn, he turned his attention to the other more recent patterns.

A group of people probably dancing? Yes, it appeared to be that, fairly easy to make out despite Grandma's rough work. And a lot of thin tree branches, it seemed, working their way into the scene. No, vines, he amended. They had to be vines, judging from the way they vaguely seemed to wrap around things and crawl over surfaces. Even in a world of magic, trees wouldn't be doing what vines did, at least insofar as Quinn's acceptance of fantastical elements and forces was concerned.

He couldn't figure out how and where she was getting these startling patterns and forms, and he wasn't convinced that Bethany existed in any way, shape, or form, either. Nowhere on the fabric had she marked patterns with a pencil, indicating a more careful and thoughtful planning of her work. Everything was simply sewn as inspiration struck her, and that idea alone stunned Quinn.

"Holy shit, Grandma," he whispered, gently laying the tapestry back on her and straightening up. "You're amazing. Weird, but amazing."

Grandma thanked him with another blast of a foghorn and what sounded suspiciously like a muttered expletive.

"Love you, too."

Quinn tiptoed to the kitchen and lost himself in breakfast, the realization that it was his day off adding a bit of happy juice to his quiet meal. His thoughts flew back to the free-standing mirror the previous night, and when at first he was back to wondering if what he'd seen was nothing but a pretty spectacular trick of an exhausted mind (further fueled by disappointment and hurt), his gut told him otherwise. As expected, the mirror revealed just his plain old self that morning, and he didn't regret not staying up longer to see what could possibly happen next. The attic room didn't look or feel different, either, which negated any simmering conspiracy theories about the otherworld somehow finding a way to leach into his world.

"Jesus. Maybe it's a virginity thing."

He sighed and rolled his eyes at himself, a cloud of grumpy gloom now looming above him as he washed his dishes and pondered the bleak wasteland he called his love life. A few dates leading to a good deal of necking and mutual handjobs back in high school, but no one had yet to knock on the back door with tongue, finger, or cock. He hadn't even experienced a single blowjob, which he'd always considered to be his most embarrassing secret of all. Was it him? Did he smell? Did he give off the wrong vibes? Maybe he cursed too much, and he was doomed to fall in love with absolute goody-two-shoes types who found male chastity belts pretty romantic.

On the other hand, there was also the issue surrounding twenty-something ne'er-do-wells who'd taken it on themselves to toy with his humanity for—whatever insensitive gain they aimed for. Quinn, now that he'd allowed a full night's sleep to pass unhindered by romantic angst and tears on his pillow, felt a great deal better and more hopeful that morning, his ability to bounce back from yesterday's mortification rendering even himself slightly mute from astonishment. He'd been on, what, four unsuccessful dates now since his return home? Yes, four. And he was now determined to make sure that numbered flatlined at four.

He paused in his task and pursed his lips. "Where the hell was I going with that?" he muttered. "God, even when I'm all alone with my thoughts, I get all scattered and shit. Oh—oh, yeah. Virginity. Weird images in the mirror. Frustrated hormones making me see all kinds of things."

Grandma was still out cold when he finished, which could only mean she'd stayed up far too late with her sewing. Quinn scrounged around for a pen and paper. He scribbled a hasty note letting her know where he'd gone to, and before long he was standing and scowling at the ruins of his home's crumbling conjoined twin.

The second half of the duplex looked like a classic haunted house, with crooked windows and walls that leaned at a pretty terrifying angle. The roof sported holes—no, Quinn quickly corrected himself. The roof no longer existed, with nothing left of its former humble grandeur but discolored and rotting beams. The gaping hole on the upper floor of the house's façade allowed him to glimpse those details.

He tested the door and was surprised to find it still working, though it did require some effort to turn the knob. A sudden earthy blast of air met him, making him wonder if the air flow coming from all of the possible openings in the house somehow managed to collect inside the decrepit structure despite the logical escape routes. But there it was: soil, leaf, and wood.

Quinn stepped across the cracked and dirty threshold and walked forward till he stood in what would be the living room. Yes, everything was as he'd imagined the interior to look after years of abandonment to the elements. There were no furniture left behind, not even wall decorations of any kind, which allowed him a means of exploring the house and seeking answers to some niggling questions about its history. Torn wallpaper, faded paint, cracked cement, weathered wood—plus random, sneaky weeds, mold and mildew, and thick cobwebs in more protected areas. The stairs leading up to the second floor were hopelessly broken, a good chunk of them missing, and those were the last few steps that would take him to the upper bedroom. The stairs to the attic room were still marginally intact, and Quinn could spot dangerous places where the wood had cracked, and the stairs sagged in those places. A small child could easily send the entire stairs falling to the first floor.

He stood in the living room, hands on his hips. There were no signs anywhere of a fire, or a flood, or any kind of damage caused by faulty appliances or man-made problems. The house simply appeared to have been abandoned, but the progression of its decay startled Quinn. The duplex wasn't that old, he knew. It was only thirty years old if his memory served him correctly, based on what his father had told him about his parents' house-hunting adventures back in the day.

The structure in its current state reminded Quinn of those photos he'd seen of rotting shells of forgotten barns or cottages or structures built out in the middle of nowhere. If anything, this house looked even worse than those pictures.

Something in the back of his mind stirred. A subtle, voiceless nudge of some sort, alerting him to something even more startling.

Silence.

Absolute silence.

It was, of course, technically impossible, given the duplex's proximity to the street and its neighbors and this house's hole-riddled structure. Noise from outside should easily be heard, and even a breeze should be felt. Quinn looked up to find the bright, cloudless sky above, but it felt as though he stood inside an eerie vacuum. The only other thing worth noting was the smell of earth pervading his immediate surroundings. Naturally, he found no holes in the floor that would have allowed soil or any other organic matter to fill the air with the smell of soil. Even the occasional hints of leaves and wood were easily noted as he sniffed, but there weren't enough of either in the ruins of the house to explain the amount that seemed to be mixed in with that of earth. All scents existed independently of the world—or of reality. It seemed as though they'd been caught in the same noiseless, movement-free bubble Quinn now found himself in.

And perhaps the most disturbing thought crossing his mind over these observations was the illogical notion that there was something distinctly alive about the vacuum. That it was, itself, a sentient being, quiet and watchful and content to observe—at least for now.

Quinn's skin broke out in goosebumps, and he immediately turned and marched back to the front door. And as expected, the moment he stepped outside, reality bore down on him quite hard, nearly making him stagger back a few steps from the sudden onslaught of noise, smell, and sensation.

"Holy shit," he breathed once he'd gathered himself. He glanced back and eyed the front door in bug-eyed shock. "I—think I know what I'm going to do on my day off now."

Not terribly fun, but still better than mourning his non-existent love life, he was forced to concede.

Nudging his glasses up his nose, he turned around and sprinted away, his mind bent on one thing only, and before long he was hurrying down Dolores's civic center, where the public library stood in all its moldy brick glory. He easily claimed a computer, and for the next several moments, he was lost in scouring the 'net for something, anything, about the duplex and its history.

# Chapter 5

The bookstore was closed one day out of the week (required mental health day and an escape from the only other employee, according to Edwin), so the first thing Quinn did after stopping by the library was to announce himself at Edwin and Tess's doorstep. The pair lived in a two-bedroom second-floor apartment in downtown Dolores, a surprising decision on their parts to rent rather than buy, given their thriving businesses. Quinn had long given up sorting out Edwin's bizarre thought processes, however, and was rather happy letting things go, especially since the apartment complex the Aguinaldos went for was one of those vintage ones with a rich history, all dolled up and improved for near-maximum luxury for renters willing to cough up big bucks for a unit.

A big, effusive grin that threatened to tear his facial muscles beyond help appeared to have lost its potency as Edwin answered the door looking as though he'd just sucked on a lemon.

"Christ, I can't get rid of you, can I?"

"Hello there, fearless leader."

"Boss."

"Yeah. Same difference. Hey, I think I figured out what's happening to Grandma." Quinn presented the folder of printed articles with a proud flourish. "Is Tess home today?"

Edwin's lemon-sucking look didn't even ease when his attention fell on Quinn's research. "The hell? Where've you been, and why are you wasting trees like this? And, no, Tess is at work."

"I've just been to the library, and I didn't have anything else on me when I decided to go there—except my wallet and keys. Besides, this was all totally spontaneous."

"You could've emailed yourself a shitload of links and then accessed them on your own computer. Boom. Done. Lots of trees and money saved. You'd better be recycling that pile of yours when you're done with it."

Quinn sighed. "Edwin, let me in. Seriously. I can't tell Grandma all of this yet, so I need to pick your brain about it and figure out what to do." He shrugged and blushed. "Well—besides forcing us both to move out because there's no way we can afford to do that, and Dad's going to kill me if we did, and our house is paid off already, so it'll be a pretty dumb idea to move out in the first place even if the house attached to ours makes me think of a dead conjoined twin."

Edwin stepped back and waved him in. "You're rambling and going all over the place again. That's some bad crack you're on, man. Go on. Get inside."

Quinn gratefully entered, greeted the Aguinaldo kids—Tom and Jerry—by giving the two big ginger cats chin rubs, and then plopped himself down on the couch that Edwin indicated with a very emphatic pointed finger, a scowl, and a grunt.

"You've eaten anything yet?" Edwin demanded.

"Yeah. I had a pastry and some coffee to jack up my blood sugar levels before I got here."

"Good. Because I ain't feeding your pasty, bony ass." Edwin sat down next to Quinn with another grunt. "Right. What's up?"

Quinn immediately spread out the sheets of text he'd printed on the coffee table. One of the cats—Quinn could never tell which one as both wore similar collars—took that as an invitation to jump on the table, sniff the paper, and plant himself on one page. And from there on, Quinn was treated to a good deal of highly inappropriate and unimpeded views of feline anus as the cat indulged in what could only be described as an hour-long tongue bath and crotch-worship.

"So—I think it's our house that's messing with Grandma's head. I went to the library to do some research on the duplex, and it's like—man, I never knew how much was written about it." Quinn waved at the sheets of paper in no small awe. "Fifty years and counting."

Edwin sighed and motioned for him to continue while the second ginger cat jumped on his lap and almost immediately melted in a ball of red, warm fur and purring muscle while Edwin petted him.

"So the duplex was built fifty years ago, not thirty like we've always thought."

"Wait—you mean the real estate agent who sold you guys your house lied about it?" Edwin blinked. "That's kind of illegal, isn't it?"

Quinn scratched his head and shrugged. "Well—I really don't know, to be honest. I *thought* we were told thirty years, but I could be misremembering everything. I mean I was too young, anyway, and we never really talked 'shop' about the house. We just moved in and made it our own. At any rate, if the real estate agent messed with us with a lie, it's a little too late to do anything about it, right? That house is already paid for. Anyway..."

Apparently the now-ruined half of the duplex had had a pretty sordid history. Since the beginning, that house had been difficult to sell because no one could live in it long enough. Terrified homeowners—or ex-homeowners—reported all kinds of hallucinations while living there. Hallucinations that apparently began around a week of them moving in.

Edwin frowned. "Hallucinations? What kind?"

"Well—shadows, sounds, movements that people kind of sense or feel, but there's no one there. Um..." Quinn frowned as he carefully searched the printout he held. "Okay, no smells or touches. Just basically visual and auditory hallucinations, but nothing specific's ever been described. Like, for instance, no one could describe the shadows or sounds in detail."

"Okay, so—ghosts, then."

"Paranormal experts claimed ghosts, yeah, but sorcerers who were called to read the place said the duplex—or the messed up half of it—straddles two worlds. Get this, Edwin. They said it's got one foot, so to speak, in an otherworld, but they didn't know what it was. Like they couldn't really figure out what was there to begin with even with all their magic stuff and so on. And it's because of that the place shouldn't be touched or messed with."

"Sorcerers were hired to read the place? For sure? Doesn't sound like whoever hired them didn't get their money's worth."

"Well—we don't really know the full story, do we? They might've been student sorcerers or scammy, under-the-table types who wouldn't know a real ghost if it haunted their ass holes."

Edwin snorted. "Doesn't matter. Sorcerers are supposed to be really good at reading shit like this. I mean I know some sorcerers, and reading houses or buildings is like one of the most basic things they learn to do in magic school or whatever school they go to for training." He waved a dismissive hand at the printouts. "It's just weird that these ones couldn't even be sure what kind of beings inhabit the world they talked about."

"That was years ago, dude. I'm sure legitimate sorcerers nowadays are a hell of a lot more knowledgeable and way better at the whole mojo-casting thing. You've got to admit, though, that's some pretty creepy stuff."

Quinn's skin crawled at the revelation, the unease he first felt upon discovering the sorcerers' reading of the property stirring again. His mind flew back to his time spent in that house's decaying shell earlier, and he finally understood what the bizarre sensory experiences he had meant. Had it been someone else claiming the whole otherworld thing, he would have easily dismissed it. But sorcerers belonged to a different species altogether as far as he was concerned, regardless of skill levels and expertise. While he never knew a sorcerer personally, he'd been keeping up with all the stories he could find about their magical history, traditions, the saints and deities who helped define their work, and especially their adventures. Sorcerers terrified Quinn, and yet he marveled at their remarkable and unique abilities.

He shared his earlier exploration of the house with Edwin, and the two discussed the significance of all those sensory anomalies Quinn had observed.

"And what's this?"

Quinn blinked and realized his mind had started to wander. He found Edwin taking one of his printouts and reading it with eyes that grew exponentially the lower they traveled on the page.

"Uh—okay, this is some pretty jacked up shit. And you live next door to this?" Edwin practically screeched.

"I know, right?"

Edwin had just read the account of the most recent owners of the doomed property—a young couple with a seven-month-old baby. They'd purchased the house at a shockingly low price, and for a little while nothing alarming was reported. That said, there'd been rumors about the father being an abusive sort, with neighbors claiming occasional fights they'd overheard between the couple. The people who lived in the house currently occupied by Quinn's family had called the police on the pair and eventually moved out, most likely because they'd grown tired of the noise and the trouble happening next door.

Then tragedy struck one day, with the husband reportedly killing his wife during a fight—he'd hit her hard and sent her falling down the stairs, breaking her neck perhaps even before she reached the landing. The baby disappeared, leading everyone to suspect the worst, and the husband's mind broke. He was found cowering inside the attic room, babbling and crying, and he was locked away in an institution. And there he died a year later. Nothing of the poor little boy was found, and the house remained empty since.

The family—Howard and Elizabeth Ann Sullivan and their baby, Keaton—apparently moved a great deal, perhaps to avoid trouble nipping at their heels, thanks to Howard's temper. And by all accounts, poor Elizabeth Ann was a quiet, mousy young woman who'd ticked off all the boxes describing the classic characteristics of a battered wife. That little Keaton had managed to survive his mother's pregnancy and first few months of life was testament enough to his mother's loving instinct to protect him despite their terrible living situation.

Elizabeth Ann. Bethany for short, Quinn thought, a quiet thrill surging through him at the realization.

Edwin appeared as though his own brain was about to give out. The lemon-sucking look had returned, but this time, it had about it a distinct edge of despair. He massaged his forehead with the heel of his hand as though it were a magical move designed to bless him with greater understanding of the deepest mysteries of the universe.

"You guys live next door to that place," he said again in a voice that could only be described as a semi-wail. "Why the hell do you still live there? Is that house keeping you enslaved or something?"

Quinn hesitated, not knowing how to break the bad news. Or creepy news, at least to him. "Well—um—not sure, exactly."

"Okay, you'd better not be hitting me with some crackhead version of *The Twilight Zone,* man."

"Sorry, dude, but—yeah. See, according to what I dug up, our house was empty for a while. But it wasn't because people didn't want to live next door to a haunted otherworld house that was now totally cursed with murder. The thing is that people couldn't live there."

Quinn immediately searched through the rest of his printouts.

"What was it? Hallucinations again?"

"Uh—no, not really." Quinn found the sheet and pounced on it. "Here you go. Not hallucinations this time. Apparently people claimed the house didn't want them."

When Edwin merely stared at him, slack-jawed and glassy-eyed, Quinn plunged ahead.

"Then my parents came, and I was still a little kid at that time, and the weird thing is, nothing kept them from moving in. If anything, I remember my mom telling me about that before she died. And it was like—she was really convinced about it and was even okay with it. You know, happy about that fact."

And if Quinn remembered correctly, his mother's pleasure had absolutely nothing to do with finding a home to settle down in, but, rather, the privilege of being—chosen—by the house itself, yet another hint pointing at her never-fully-tapped psychic abilities. Again, nothing but silence met Quinn's account.

"I didn't think too much about it then, but now—I don't know. She said the house let them move in because it wanted our family there. Like it'd been vetting family after family for a while before deciding that we were the right ones, and it let us buy it and move in without trouble. It took about seven years after what happened next door for it to find us—sort of."

And by that time, the house next door had already been reduced to the rotting shell of its former self.

"And how's all this supposed to be affecting your grandmother?"

Quinn grimaced. "I think the house is trying to talk to her or something. It's nuts, but something tells me this is what's really happening."

Edwin sighed and slapped the coffee table, startling the cat on his lap, and it jumped off. "Okay, that's it. I'm going to warm up some leftover *palabok*. Got some flan in the fridge, too. You can take some of that home. This crazy shit is making me hungry, and I've got to feed your pasty, bony ass now that you're here. If Tess found out I didn't fatten you up with all that food in the fridge, she'd murder me dead."

# Chapter 6

"Quinn? Are you sick or something?"

"Hmm? Me? No, Grandma. Just—um—appreciating the wall." Quinn caught himself too late, and he sighed, pinching his eyes shut and shaking his head at himself. "That was pretty dumb," he muttered.

Grandma snorted as she hobbled past him, carrying a small pile of clean towels toward the kitchen. "A wall is a wall is a wall, kid. Unless you suddenly see blood pouring down ours, there's nothing there worth all that eyeball strain."

She disappeared in the kitchen, and before long the usual calm of their home was broken by her shrill, two-note whistling. Quinn ignored everything around him as he bent all thought on the wall the house shared with the haunted one next door. He felt at a loss as to what, exactly, it was he was hoping to find because after several seconds of staring long and hard at the same three-foot radius and getting nothing for his pains, he was getting more and more convinced this was all a really stupid idea.

Well, in truth, he'd already known that, stopping before a random section of the living room wall and mulling over what he'd just learned about his home's history. Mulling turned into glassy-eyed staring and then baffled, self-conscious observing. And, of course, the longer he stood there, questioning his decision to just—stand and stare—at a section of a wall, the worse he felt about himself.

What was he expecting to find, anyway?

Weird symbols carved into the wood? Sigils, maybe? The kind that appeared only when the moonlight struck the wall at a certain angle? Faces leering at him, all the while being cleverly hidden among the wood grain patterns? Figures creeping along the length of the wall, following him from room to room?

So far, nothing. Just boring wood and its boring aging and boring veneer long fading into boring weathered surfaces.

"Jesus, how redundant is that?"

"I told you, didn't I? Get with the program, sonny, or I'm going to have to call a psychiatrist on you," Grandma said in what could only be described as a long-suffering tone as she moved past him again, heading back to her bedroom. When she disappeared inside, she called out, "You'll talk to me if you've got issues, right, Quinn? I know I'm not your mother, bless her poor little soul, but I managed to raise your father and survive the trauma. That's qualification enough in my eyes for any psych help you might need from a concerned member of the family."

Quinn merely gazed at her open bedroom door with a thinly pinched mouth. "Hey, Grandma? Have you ever heard Mom or Dad say something weird about how they got the house?"

Grandma didn't answer right away as the sounds of banging doors and sliding drawers momentarily peppered the silence. "I think your mom mentioned something about the house wanting them to move in—or some creepy-ass shit like that."

"You mean like the house rejected everyone else and chose them? Something like that?" Quinn suddenly realized he still held the folder of printouts against his chest. He definitely needed to spend more time on them, even go back online to cross-reference information if he could. His poor old laptop was in for a thorough beating that night.

"Yeah—something like that," Grandma replied with a heavy sigh. "I thought at first she was pregnant again and was hopped up on hormones, but it turned out to be something worse. She just developed a fixation on—I know I'm repeating myself here—some creepy-ass shit."

Grandma presently appeared carrying another pile of clean towels.

"Did she ever tell you or Dad where she got the idea from?" Quinn barely took note of Grandma as she hobbled past him again in the direction of the kitchen.

"No, I don't think so. If she did, I must've blocked it out of my memory because it'd be too much disturbing crap for my geriatric brain to handle."

Grandma disappeared in the kitchen, and like before, she filled the quiet with her two-note, off-key whistling. "Oh, Quinn? I've run out of towels. I guess you should call a plumber and tell him we have a potential flood problem in the kitchen, and terrycloth towels don't make good dikes. Be a darling sweetheart, that's my good boy."

* * * *

While the plumber kept Grandma busy downstairs, Quinn took advantage of the time to sort through his printouts again, his head throbbing as information seemed to come hard and fast at him—worse than when he was first in the library and then at Edwin's.

He scrubbed his face with both hands.

"God," he muttered. "Why am I suddenly getting dragged into this? All this time I've lived here—why now?"

He'd been thinking about that point on and off since visiting the library—of how everything strange had been happening recently and in quick succession. As if events he'd yet to find out about, let alone understand, were coming to a head. But what, how, and especially why?

He froze when a thought struck him. An anniversary. Was that it? Was it the anniversary of that woman's murder? Quinn swallowed as goosebumps broke out all over, and he quickly searched for dates once he pulled out the news accounts of the murder from his scattered collection of information.

And there it was.

"Holy shit," he whispered. His mind raced as he stared in helplessness and disbelief at the printout. "Okay, granted the anniversary won't be for another seven months, but still—things seem to get weirder and weirder, and they're happening faster and faster, the closer we get. Uh—might be a pretty nutty coincidence, though." Something deep in his gut insisted nothing had anything to do with coincidence, however. "But—if that's the case, why didn't any of these bizarre things happen before?"

Through the years of his family's residence there, not once did Quinn feel or experience anything out of the ordinary. No hallucinations as described by those who'd tried to live in the house next door. His mother's eerie claim regarding their success in getting the house never even registered in Quinn's mind as anything other than silly, mundane stuff.

"It happened on the year I was born, too," he murmured, frowning at the printouts now lying in a widely spaced mess on his bed. "Unless Mom and Dad made a deal with some messed-up fairies and I'm actually a changeling, I don't know how else..."

He paused and made a face. How did sorcerers sort out puzzles involving magic, immortals, the otherworld, dead people, ghosts, demons, etc.? Quinn knew next to nothing about the true nature and level of complexity of a sorcerer's world and especially their calling. Bits of information gleaned from books, yes, and some information—however questionable—from the internet, but nothing more than that. Quinn had to admit rather sheepishly that his fascination with magic and all things darkly fantastic had led him to his current job, and there he'd limited his scope.

He now surrounded himself with merchandise that was both kitschy and ridiculous for the casual collectors and symbolically significant for true believers and even amateur practitioners of some form of magic or pagan religion. Harmless stuff on the whole for laymen who didn't have the right qualities for a career in sorcery. In many ways, he'd been hawking objects that were almost a mockery of the true nature of magic, objects designed by enterprising know-nothings for superficial consumption.

That said, was magic logical? Did everything cast in shadow and living side-by-side with the sunlit world of ordinary people follow its own laws of physics? Quinn figured it did, but it was also not bound by what everyone else believed to be logical as humanity defined it. Perhaps magic was chaos redefined, and the only thing keeping it from breaching the walls and pouring right into the world of mortals was the ever-present army of strictly vetted and highly trained sorcerers. Quinn couldn't help a shudder at the thought.

"I wonder how..."

Quinn let out a startled yelp and turned, his sudden movement sending some of the printouts flying off the bed. Shadows again—furtive movements in the periphery of his vision. When he turned, he was once again staring at the mirror.

"Oh, hell, not again!"

As before, the image in the mirror was of that strange room. Quinn pulled his glasses off, knuckled his eyes, and then put them back on.

"Nope, still there." He glanced at the windows and then his wrist watch. "So I'm getting weird things happening in my own bedroom during the day now? Hauntings don't happen at midnight or when the moon's up and stuff? How *fun*."

Initial surprise and nervousness eased into cautious curiosity, and Quinn carefully scooted over to the edge of the bed and stood up. Keeping his gaze fixed on the mirror, he walked toward it as though entranced by its shadowy world. And in a way, he was.

A cold spot had taken residence directly in front of the mirror, making Quinn wince at the sudden bubble of chilly air. He rubbed his arms for warmth, a touch of surprise coursing through him when he caught sight of his breaths coming out in faint clouds.

"Okay, you can do this. You can do this," he murmured, squaring his shoulders and centering himself before taking the final steps closer to the mirror.

No fear gripped him the entire time following the initial surprise over the cold spot. If anything, something he couldn't see calmed him from some strange distance or place. Quinn blinked when he mentally put two and two together, his gaze falling on the mirror after a quick and questioning glance around him.

No, there was definitely no fear gripping him.

Only a quiet, gentle urging coming from the mirror's world, a voiceless call that found its way into his head and one that had about it an edge of desperate hope, unless Quinn was simply reading too much into a moment that was obviously supernatural in origin. There was also something almost—maternal—about that quiet summoning. A motherly coaxing Quinn had experienced a hundred times in the past from his own mother.

He stopped in front of the mirror and regarded the strange room within in some anticipation. Nothing was happening there, and if Quinn were honest with himself, he'd sooner not have anything else take place in the mirror's world, or he'd surely soil his pants.

That voiceless urging returned. Wait, please, it seemed to say. Please—he shouldn't go, at least not yet. He needed to have a little more patience.

Quinn blinked. "For what? I waited last time, and nothing happened."

He needed to allow things to happen as the Fates intended. Time was of the essence, yes, but patience was still a necessity for the prescribed pattern to reveal itself. Happiness was at stake—happiness, freedom, and devotion meant to last a lifetime if Fortune were to favor any decision he made from this crucial point onward.

Quinn scowled now, utterly mystified. "Huh? Decisions? What?" Another idea seized him, and he whispered, "Bethany? Is—is that you?"

The strange presence in his head—there was simply no other way to describe it—seemed to laugh or chuckle at that. Yes, it was Bethany. Yes, she was real. A brief pause followed and then...

Yes, she was alive once.

Before Quinn could recover from the shock of that revelation, movement from inside the mirror caught his attention, and he couldn't help the loud yelp of surprise that burst out of him as well as the his instinctive shrinking away from the mirror. His eyes, large in disbelief, were now fixed on the figure of a young man in old-fashioned dress, who stared back at Quinn with equal shock, his mouth hanging open.

# Chapter 7

"Oh, fuck me twice, it's James Steerforth," Quinn breathed once he managed to get his vocal cords to function again.

If any embarrassing secret could be tortured out of Quinn Geiger, it would be his overheated swooning over a fictional character. Well—it would actually count as one of several embarrassing secrets pertaining to fictional characters if Quinn were to be painfully honest about it. He'd rather not be, of course, since admitting to those meant staring right into the abyss of why he'd yet to be deflowered by the love of his life.

The young man in the mirror appeared to recover from his shock with a start, followed by wide-eyed blinking and then a softly exhaled word that Quinn didn't catch. Quinn didn't know if the oddly dressed—but utterly delectable—young man spoke English.

The silence stretched for a bit following their recovery from shock, with Quinn nudging his glasses up even as he inched closer to the mirror, his mind racing after ideas on how best to break the—pretty surreal—ice. In the end he decided the direct approach was the best one to take.

"Um—hi," he stammered, raising a hand tentatively. "How's it going?"

Young Mr. Quasi-Steerforth gave another start, but this time, obviously encouraged, he strode confidently to the mirror and then smiled at Quinn. And Quinn, for his part, suddenly remembered another reason as to why he'd yet to be deflowered by the love of his life: physical beauty. A niggling detail involving his absolute lack of, one now being broadcast into the bizarre and eerie world the stranger inhabited. Or at least in the face of astonishing male beauty, Quinn grew more acutely aware of his own physical deficiencies.

He immediately and instinctively hunched, bringing his shoulders up as though to protect his ears and then curling them forward while crossing his arms tightly and shuffling from foot to foot.

"Oh, good, you speak English," the young man said, still smiling. He radiated confidence in the most ridiculously attractive way possible, and Quinn suddenly regretted encouraging the conversation. "Hello back. What's your name?"

"Quinn? Quinn Geiger?"

"Are you sure?"

"Yeah—yeah, I'm sure. That—that's my name. Uh—yeah."

"Excellent! It's nice to meet you, Quinn Geiger. I'm Keaton."

Oh, no. Oh, nonononononononono.

Time seemed to stand still, encasing Quinn in a thick bubble of cold yet oddly solid air, constricting his chest and forcing him to stop breathing for a fraction of a second. The shock, a sudden blow that sent him psychically flying and striking an invisible wall somewhere, rendered him speechless. It couldn't be Keaton, he thought, and he swore his brain's voice actually wailed in horror. Not *the* Keaton Sullivan of tragic note.

And yet—and *yet*—it all made too much damned sense. It was only a matter of logistics insofar as how in heaven's name Keaton ended up in the mirror's world like this.

*Don't panic. Don't even think of panicking. She led you here. See where all this takes you.*

A handful of seconds' worth of mental slapping helped him find his center, and he took a breath to clear away the shock. How did one go about testing the waters, anyway? It wouldn't do to startle Keaton any further with odd behavior or an overly direct and blunt line of questioning. Best to move forward cautiously, he appended.

Quinn waited, allowing a pause to run its course, then prodded in all pretend innocence, "Keaton—what? Smith?"

"No. Just Keaton."

Keaton beamed a great, big, beautiful smile that made his face glow, imbuing it with complete, knee-weakening beauty. Quinn could only stiffen and double down on his painfully self-conscious posture and attitude.

"But don't you have a surname?"

Keaton shrugged. "If I do, I've no idea what it is."

The back-and-forth debate over blurting out the truth regarding Keaton's surname was brief and frenzied, but caution won out since Quinn was still too unsure of the nature of Keaton's entrapment, let alone true mental state. He didn't even know if Keaton was nothing more than a ghost at this point and not a warm-blooded mortal considering how long he'd been in the mirror's world.

"Oh. That's weird."

"Like your outfit? It's a little skimpy from where I'm standing."

Quinn had to glance down and take quick stock: a medium-weight t-shirt, skinny jeans, and socks. His sneakers sat against the wall next to his wardrobe, and his thin cotton hoodie lay in a crumpled mass on his bed. He looked up and met intense brown eyes that seemed determined to drill a hole through his skull.

"It's standard modern day stuff—pretty practical and comfortable. Now what *you're* wearing's a little out there." Quinn caught himself quickly enough. "I'm not saying your clothes suck because they don't, and they really make you look, uh, pretty goddamn hot. But—you speak English and sound pretty modern, yet you're dressed in clothes from two hundred years ago, and your bedroom's kind of—creepy. I mean—what's with the vines and the worn out look? Like your room's about to fall apart when a storm hits. It also looks like my room's alternate universe alter ego, especially where the furniture's placed and stuff."

The filter wasn't working, and Quinn realized it too late. He'd ignored his family whenever they pointed out how "babbly" he was whenever he was uncomfortable, which often happened when caught doing something he wasn't supposed to, and said habit had been pinged as a major indicator of a guilty conscience. This time, though, he was simply uncomfortable, full stop, being smack dab in the middle of a pretty tangled situation involving a magical world, a terribly handsome mortal (who might not be mortal anymore) trapped within, and, quite sadly, being the conversation partner of the very same terribly handsome mortal (who might not be mortal anymore).

"Well, I know how to speak English because I'm human, and I was raised by people who pretty much, uh, understood what I'm all about—or where I really came from. They've been from your world at one point, anyway, and they spent years there. They're mightily hard to impress, I find, and they're pretty set in their ways, but they took care of me as best as they could."

Keaton paused, appearing to give Quinn's surroundings a cursory glance before pinning Quinn back in place with his incredibly intense gaze.

Or was it intense? Keaton's conversation seemed to veer very slightly off the path here and there, as though he were distracted easily by one thing or another, and his mind couldn't quite keep the goal in sight. Now that he stood close enough to Quinn for a clearer impression, Quinn realized there was a decidedly dreamy haze in Keaton's eyes, lovely though they might be. It was a peculiar, glassy quality that revealed a mind lost in a dream even if Keaton still managed to converse pretty easily with him.

Keaton stood the way every Victorian gentleman stood in those handful of historical dramas Quinn had devoured as a teen: elegantly relaxed with his hands held behind him, one leg bent with its foot turned out. If Quinn could swoon into Keaton's arms without looking like a damned fool, he would.

Something jarred Quinn out of his starry-eyed reverie. "Wait, what? People? There are people there?"

"I really don't know what this place is officially called, and I've asked around," Keaton piped up, glancing around him this time. He shrugged again. "I was told it's a world that's the mirror image of yours, and, well, obviously it is, now that I'm looking at it. Only difference is that this place is all magic. As far as my last name goes, I wasn't given one. Those who raised me said 'Keaton' was all they got, and they just made do. It doesn't really matter, anyway. They took care of me, and I've got no real complaints. Other than—dreams, I guess. Lots of them. I think I spend more time dreaming than being awake and talking."

"Dreams? You—sleep a lot? Or they make you sleep a lot over there?"

"I suppose. I've never really questioned my day-to-day living here. If anything, events just blend into each other, and they blend into my dreams as well. It's—pretty interesting on the whole." Keaton suddenly chuckled and shrugged. "I baptized this world unofficially since I need to have an easy name to remember, so now I refer to it as Glass-Dreams."

Keaton's easy confidence seemed to falter when he spoke the last sentence, the light in his eyes dimming a little, his smiling features momentarily falling into shadow and doubt. The shift was too subtle and too quick for Quinn to really, fully catch on and make something of, however, so he forced himself to cautiously file the observation away in case it proved to be valuable eventually.

At the same time, Quinn's addled brain had been frantically chasing after so many fragments all at once the whole time Keaton talked. It seemed like having a gigantic puzzle get blown to bits, and he was running around in a desperate attempt at catching all the flying ruins in his hands.

He noticed, now that Keaton had revealed more bits about his life in Glass-Dreams, how thin Keaton really was. His cheekbones showed, there was a boniness to his figure despite the layers of clothes so typical of a Victorian gentleman, and those made Quinn wonder about sustenance and just how people in that world were able to keep Keaton alive. He certainly seemed healthy enough, given he was still upright and breathing and functioning quite normally despite the occasional quirks. But the thought of nutrition and care and the possibility that Keaton was actually starving to death over there made Quinn's stomach turn.

"Okay," he stammered, the need to shrink into himself in miserable self-consciousness now getting overrun by shock and curiosity. "That's all right. So—your clothes."

"These? Got nothing else to wear. Everyone else here wears the same thing, you know. They told me it's been just like this forever, though people here wear a wide variety of styles of clothes. Some look kind of tacky and garish with the wigs, but more of my friends look like me." Keaton's smile turned lopsided and playful. "You're really beautiful. It looks like you try to use your glasses like a shield, but you're not fooling me. And you've got those—those—marks on your nose and a few on your cheeks."

Quinn couldn't help a grimace as he blushed, shifting his weight from foot to foot more emphatically. Apparently he wasn't the only one with an issue with filters. "They're called freckles. I don't know where I got them from." He trailed his fingers over his cheeks and saw Keaton's eyes follow his hands' movements. "I mean—my mom had crazy porcelain skin, and my dad's got no freckles, either."

And speaking of parentage...

"Do you—do your parents still live?" Quinn prodded quickly before Keaton could get a word in.

"No. I never knew them."

"I'm so sorry. But—how'd you end up there if you're mortal?"

Keaton's smile wavered for a moment as he considered, but his easy, friendly manner was back swiftly enough. "The story is that I was a foundling. You know, an abandoned child."

Not once in Quinn's life did he expect to hear "foundling" used in modern conversation, and he found himself suitably impressed. All the same, he had the worst time tamping down his nervous energy as he mentally played detective. All those puzzle pieces were now falling neatly into place and yet not, too many pieces still eluding his grasp and taunting him relentlessly, and he hoped he wouldn't forget a single word spoken during this extraordinary exchange. He'd already pinched himself to make sure he was, indeed, awake and lucid through-out all this.

"And—are you living with fairy folk or something?"

Keaton's face brightened considerably. "That's a funny question. No, they're people. Just ordinary people."

"Ah. Okay, never mind."

"I love your sense of humor. I should have you meet some of my friends here. I'm sure they'll absolutely love you."

Quinn shrank back a couple of steps, eyes widening in horror. "Nope. You're not going to mojo me into your world. I'm fine with my world and my kind of pathetic social circle, thanks."

"Mojo? Oh, magic? I'm mortal. I don't do magic, but my friends are good at it," Keaton replied, all innocence and openness in his manner. Then he stepped closer to the mirror and placed both of his hands against it, a palpable wave of yearning suddenly pouring out of him as he kept his dream-clouded eyes glued on Quinn. "If I did—if I could do magic—I'd go to your world instead. At least there I know I can age with everyone, not watch those around me stay young and healthy while I grow old, get sick, and die."

Keaton's voice had dropped to a near whisper when he spoke, and he sounded as though he were confiding a long-suppressed secret with a sympa-thetic friend. Quinn wasn't sure if it was nothing more than one of a billion tricks of the mind, but for a fleeting second, the glassy quality of Keaton's gaze seemed vanish when he spoke. But it *was* fleeting, and before Quinn could make up his mind, the dreamy haze was back.

Quinn closed the gap as well, unable to resist the urge to touch some of the magic that currently kept him and Keaton apart despite their proximity to each other. Summoning his courage, Quinn pressed his hands against the mirror as well, ensuring that each hand met its Glass-Dreams partner. And with a start, he felt a hint of warmth from the contact, leaving him to wonder if the magic holding Keaton in the mirror's world was, in some way, malleable enough to be breached if he were to help Keaton cross over to the mortal world. Perhaps with Bethany's help?

Keaton blushed at the contact, and he smiled—a distracted, distant one, at that. "Would you mind pressing your mouth to the glass so I can kiss you?"

And, unsurprisingly, it was at that very moment when the spell broke. Keaton and his eerie world faded in mere seconds, the sudden look of vague anguish on his face being the very last image Quinn had of him.

# Chapter 8

"Holy shit, Edwin...I just...I can't..."

"You want to take an extra ten and calm down? I think you should. You're freaking out our customers."

Quinn glanced around the store—easy enough to do with his bird's eye view of the place, standing near the top rung of the ladder in order to replenish stock on the uppermost shelves. Rolling his eyes, he frowned at Edwin, who stood by the opposite wall and was practically dwarfed by boxes of newly shipped merchandise.

"Edwin, there's no one here."

"I know. Because they're all gone. You freaked them all out with your crazy-ass babbling, and the—you know, it sucks when I have to explain a sarcastic swipe. It's no better than explaining a joke, and it kind of defeats of the purpose of doing it in the first place," Edwin retorted. Then he sighed and motioned Quinn down with a tired wave of a hand. "Come down from there, man. You're making me nervous. Just limit yourself to stocking lower shelves while sorting through your haunted house issues."

He paused, considering. Then came the *coup de grace*.

"I've got some slices of mocha cake for you. Tess told me to bring some extra to help you bulk up."

"Mocha cake? You're shitting me."

"Nope. You can have some if you come down from that ladder in one piece."

Quinn didn't need any more persuading. Tongue practically hanging out of his mouth, he scrambled down the ladder, miraculously avoiding a catastrophe despite the ancient ladder's dangerous rattling and groaning in answer to his frantic movements. Before long he'd moved the poor, overused relic to the least visited corner of the store.

"I think I'll wait till after I help you restock some of the shelves before having some of that awesome stuff," Quinn chirped, words a little broken as he lightly panted from the greed-induced acrobatic exertions.

He ambled back to the middle of the small store, a bit shocked by how much the limited space was able to handle all those boxes in addition to the usual crammed tables and shelves.

"Dude, I'm sure Keaton's that missing baby. He's got to be. And, uh, yeah."

"Kind of stands to reason, doesn't it? How many people trapped in mirrors in your home have names that're the same as a missing baby?"

"Yeah. That was a real 'duh' moment for me. I'm still reeling from what happened, so go easy on my brain. It's threatening to retire early."

Quinn felt utterly lost as to where he wanted to take the conversation. Ever since he arrived for his shift, it had been non-stop talking, all those pent-up ideas and wildly suppressed theories suddenly exploding out of him in an endless torrent of half-coherent word salads. At least according to Edwin, who was having a pretty difficult time keeping up with Quinn's excited babbling. Quinn hadn't shared anything with Grandma yet as he needed to consult with a disinterested—or what came close to disinterested in his pathetically limited experience in social interactions and understanding of human nature—third party first before spilling the beans with her. He simply didn't know how she'd react to his supernatural experiences, what with her own ongoing close encounters with dead people who should be haunting the house next door but realized the effort would've been a lost cause.

"Well—where's all this going?" Edwin demanded. He looked at the items he held as though he only now realized they existed. "We ordered more gargoyles? When did this happen?"

"I know where that missing baby went. That's one thing. I know he's been raised by people who live in some alternate world in the mirror. He could've called them 'beings', frankly, and it wouldn't have made a lick of difference because that still would've been pretty accurate in describing who and what the hell these people are. I mean—what kind of people live in a world inside a mirror?"

Quinn regarded the pair of hefty-looking stone statues Edwin held, his brain halting momentarily.

"Oh—I think it was that day when you came in with a hangover. You know, like the day after your brother's bachelor party. You came in still wearing that cum-crisped suit you put on for that stripper bar. And those are chimeras, not gargoyles. People make that mistake all the time. Anyway, now I'm trying to figure out what to do with all these things I know." Which, really, weren't much, and they were mostly conjectures.

Edwin cursed under his breath and carefully re-boxed the unsightly and rather overly big statues. He crouched beside another open box and surveyed its contents.

"Can't be a coincidence, everything that's happened to you. I'm sure it means something, like you're being shown some kind of scenario that you need to be a part of. Just hope Keaton's not being raised by fairies because if he is, you're screwed ten different ways. But if they do turn out to be fairies, don't piss them off and make them suck you into their world. I heard that a pissed off fairy's a really messed up motherfucker, and you wouldn't want one of those coming after your ass."

Quinn considered for a moment, his mind straying to Keaton and his acceptance of his lot in life and yet confessing to a state of loneliness, being the only mortal in a world of immortals. There was that lack of a real connection with those whom he'd grown up looking to as family. Keaton appeared to be relatively fine and functional despite an alarming sign of a lack of proper nutrition and a strange distance in his gaze and a faintly distracted mind. By and large, anyway, what Quinn had seen seemed to be a display of care given to an orphaned baby who didn't fit in biologically, psychically, mentally, and so on. He also seemed relatively well-adjusted enough—though, admittedly, he'd never been exposed to other worlds and experiences till his meeting with Quinn—and having come across Quinn through magical means might endanger that.

"But what if I'm being shown all those things because I'm expected to do something about it? How can I possibly figure that one out?"

Like the "chosen one" trope he detested so much in some of the books he'd read. He'd always thought of it as a lazy way of justifying the main character's importance, which tended to be on the level of god-like. Quinn would absolutely hate his life if he were to find himself stuck in a bad trope with no convincing, logical basis for it other than "just because".

Edwin snorted and pulled out voodoo dolls—the cheap, a-dime-a-dozen, tourist trap offerings oozing from every gothic corner of New Orleans—and stared blankly at them. It was quite clear he couldn't remember ordering those, either, and Quinn dared not say a word about the circumstances behind the dolls' unexpected appearance in the store that day. He decided to wait and al-

low his baffled boss a merciful stretch of time to recover from the shock before...

Well, before telling him it was immediately after a huge family party that
Edwin stumbled, drunk and giddy, into the store just before closing time and
placed the order himself because he was feeling a tad generous. Quinn would
have protested had he not been distracted by a hunky sorcerer-type who'd been
perusing the books for some time that evening, bemusedly fielding questions
from a hopelessly infatuated Quinn regarding the otherworld and magic and
what Mr. Hunky Sorcerer liked for dinner if he were to be asked out on a date.

"Do something?" Edwin echoed, still staring at the voodoo dolls. "You
mean like rescue the dude? Like a superhero—only nerdier and scrawnier?"

"Well, if you put it that way," Quinn grumbled, glaring at Edwin. "Look, I
think he's trapped there. No, I *know* he's trapped there, and he's not even aware
of it. He doesn't act like he's freaking out or anything, and he was a little, uh,
kind of forward and blunt and socially awkward, but I'm pretty sure it's because
he's lived too long in bizarre-o land." He paused and emphatically tapped his
temple with a finger. "Those people he's with are slowly stripping away his human qualities. It's like amnesia or even dementia. That's why he's kind of out
there and has almost zero social skills. I'll bet you that's how it is."

"Zero social skills?"

"Yeah. He, uh, kind of wanted to kiss me through the mirror. I mean, who
does that?"

Edwin blinked. "Wow, that's pretty sad, even for you."

"Right?" Quinn grunted thoughtfully and gazed around the store as he
mentally scrabbled further. "He was, uh, a little distracted when he talked. You
know, he rambled a teeny-tiny bit, like his mind couldn't really focus well. There
was also this weird, glassy quality to his eyes."

"Like he's stoned?"

"Sort of, I guess. Like his mind's completely somewhere else but also lost in
something really nice. I didn't sense anything freaky at all in his behavior even
with the haziness and stuff." As though Keaton were enchanted, in fact, Quinn
mentally appended, and that was yet one more thing he needed to file away for
further perusal.

He sighed and crouched next to Edwin and gently took the voodoo dolls
out of the stiff and clammy fingers. Quinn wouldn't be surprised if Edwin was

currently semi-catatonic because his brain had fractured, and parts of it were scrambling to calculate just how much those voodoo dolls had set them back. Quinn took pity on him and awkwardly patted Edwin's shoulder.

"I'll find a spot for these. I'm sure even people in Dolores would be down for a random voodoo doll or two," he said. He carefully placed the dolls back in the box and stood up to sweep his gaze around the shop, his hands on his hips.

"Okay, so how're you supposed to rescue the guy? You gonna break the mirror and see if there's a hidden door inside it? That'll be pretty stupid, if you think about it—like cursing yourself with seven years' bad luck because the only way in and out of that world is a goddamn mirror."

Quinn glanced at Edwin, a crooked smile curving his lips. "Sounds pretty sadistic, huh? I wouldn't put it past them if Keaton's people *are* fairies, and they set things up like that. Like you said, they can be pretty messed up motherfuckers."

Edwin waved his hands before him as though warding off flies. "Okay, okay, okay. Whatever. So here's how I understand things. Creepy-ass things are happening to you more and more lately because this guy—"

"Keaton." Quinn couldn't help the sudden, awkward thrill that coursed through him at the mention of Keaton's name.

"Keaton—probably needs to be taken away from the world he's stuck in. And since you happen to sleep in the attic room, or *our* world's version of the attic room, you've been kind of chosen to do the job."

"Kind of chosen" would be the understatement of the century considering how the Geiger family got the house in the first place, Quinn groused silently as he waited for Edwin to finish his spiel.

"As to why it's happening *now,* I'm guessing it's because there's something about this time of the year that's making it all possible. Like the anniversary of Bethany's death."

Quinn picked his way past other boxes in the direction of the impulse buy section. He should be able to move a few things around, consolidate others, and clear up enough room for the voodoo dolls.

"Yeah, but why this year and not last year? Or the year before?" he demanded as he set about the task. Being forced to organize certainly had its perks, he thought, as it forced his mind to follow suit and sort things out as well. "No, I think it's the year and not the season that's important."

"Is there a way to find out Keaton's birthday? I'm thinking that might have something to do with it."

"You think so?"

Quinn fell silent and considered. He'd learned through his research that Keaton was only a few months old when tragedy struck next door, and those events took place the year Quinn was born. No, he corrected himself. He remembered the news accounts claiming that Keaton was only seven months old when he disappeared. They were, in a nutshell, the same age, with Keaton possibly being older by a few weeks, perhaps. Twenty-one, then? Was there a particular significance to that number?

"Hey, boss—you know anything about numerology?" he asked after a moment.

"No, not really. What's up?"

Quinn scratched his head and turned his gaze back to the box of voodoo dolls, his eyes seeing nothing as he pursued that thought. "Well—I was just wondering if there's something significant about years and numbers and all that's going—oh, hell, there is!" He blinked, head clearing, and he looked up to meet Edwin's baffled frown with a huge, smug grin. "Seven. Things seem to have seven worked into them somehow. Like Keaton and I are twenty-one—multiple of seven, yeah? My family was 'allowed' to buy the house after seven years of it being on the market on and off. I don't think Bethany's death anniversary has anything to do with it since that won't be for another five months or so, not seven. Keaton was seven months old when shit hit the fan. I don't think all of this is coincidence."

# Chapter 9

There were no unusual events involving magical (or cursed, depending on one's perspective, Quinn determined) mirrors for the next two days. He'd even stayed up well after his usual bed time, reading or listening to music, waiting for something to happen. The disappointment when nothing did fell somewhere between heavy and crippling, and Quinn was shocked at how much he was affected by Keaton's no-show.

One meeting, he thought. It was only one measly meeting, and yet his world had shifted off its humdrum alignment in ways that convinced him there was no going back. A new kind of normal had been defined for him, and that was simply that. Of course, he also had to remind himself that he lived in Dolores, and the world as it currently stood was steeped in magic of every stripe, with immortals, saints, Nature, and science holding sway.

Quinn sat before the mirror on the second evening, alternately glaring at his reflection and thoughtfully frowning at it. Keaton's sudden appearance had been just that: sudden. There'd been no sign, no warning of any sort, that came before the curtain separating the mortal world and that of otherworldly beings thinned.

"No, wait a minute. He showed himself to me once," Quinn whispered, frowning at the memory. "That mirror on the stairs. That was him, wasn't it?"

A cold spot had also been there simultaneously, and like the actual meeting he'd had with Keaton, that first cold spot was directly in front of the smaller mirror. It happened so quickly, though, as if Bethany—and Quinn was now convinced it was her—had decided at the spur of the moment to make Keaton's presence known to him, hence the too-brief meeting of two worlds. Like a supernatural hiccup, almost. And from what Quinn had long known about ghosts and hauntings, ghosts required an immense amount of energy in order to communicate with the living, whether as apparitions or in other ways.

Bethany must have used up all of her strength to make the lengthier face-to-face with Keaton possible. That meant it would take her longer to recover and try again.

Quinn had also gone over his printouts a few more times, cross-referencing as much information as he could online, but he continued to come up short.

The tragic history of the house next door was so simple and straightforward that nothing else but plain facts had been documented and archived.

The abusive husband's residence in the institution had been described as "mute" and "hunted", according to follow-up news reports that had spanned several weeks before interest petered out. Apparently the man hadn't spoken since his wife's death and had gone about his days burdened with so much terror that he'd acted as though he were being constantly shadowed by something no one could see. And that had been that, much to Quinn's dismay.

"Hey, Keaton? Are you there?" he called out softly and pressed a hand against the mirror. The glass stayed cold and lifeless, and he sighed at the remembrance of Keaton wanting to kiss him.

That had been a right shocker, and with the mirror's magic ending immediately after Keaton's bold—and possibly misguided—request for a kiss, Quinn was simply left with no time at all to recover and agree or disagree. Of course, he'd had enough time since to reflect on that moment, and while a tiny part of him yearned for that kiss, the rest of him had easily brushed it off, knowing Keaton could easily do better. Just like Matt and those other young men who'd stood him up in the past. Quinn knew his place well enough, and he needed to remind himself of that as often as he possibly could, or he'd overstep his bounds yet again and end up ashamed and hurt.

He also had to remind himself that this surreal adventure shouldn't be about him. It should be about Keaton and how Bethany probably wanted Quinn to get him out of Glass-Dreams before it was too late.

"It's Quinn. I'm here. I'd love to talk to you again."

He fell silent and waited, keeping his hand on the mirror in hopes it would somehow rouse the magic that kept their worlds apart. At the same time, he thought about the too-subtle revelations of Keaton's true state of mind throughout their conversation. The unexpected expressions of longing and loneliness whenever his guard went down, as though it had been held together by the barest and most fragile threads for too long.

The reason behind Keaton's sudden appearance continued to feed the fire in Quinn's belly. There was a reason for this, he told himself. Things—whether natural or supernatural—happened for a reason, and this was no exception. He'd read up more on the spiritual, cultural, mathematical, and otherworldly significance of the number seven, and he was ready to put that number aside while keeping track of its meaning as it was applied to his current adventures. Other than the label of a "perfect number" often used by different cultures and religions, there was also that curious little detail from ancient Rome and how Romans believed that the human body and soul regenerated every seven years. And how, as widely believed, the mirror reflected a person's soul.

Renewal, revival, restoration. Those, Quinn thought, held the greatest significance in his case, hence the preponderance of the mystical number he'd never given much thought to in his daily activities, at least until now.

Quinn sighed heavily and pulled his hand away. Nothing was going to happen that night, and he was in danger of spotting more and more flaws on his face despite Keaton's gushing praise of his beauty.

"Well, I really shouldn't be surprised," he muttered as he forced his gaze away and turned his attention to an ominous-looking dustbunny lurking under his bed. "If he's been trapped there since he was a baby, it's only expected that he'd consider the first warm-blooded human he meets to be good-looking."

If Keaton were to successfully leave Glass-Dreams for the mortal world, he'd be drowning in good-looking—or better-looking—people. For now his bar was set quite low with Quinn being the only standard by which Keaton could define male beauty. At least among mortals. He simply needed to see the human world more and improve his judgment, and Quinn was sure he wouldn't be anywhere within range once the dust cleared.

"Ah, bite me. I'm going to bed."

* * * *

Quinn was off work the following day, and he decided to check the status of Grandma's epic tapestry over breakfast.

"How're things coming along with your sewing, Grandma?"

"They're coming," Grandma replied, eyeing Quinn suspiciously over her coffee. "Why?"

Quinn shrugged, feigning mild disinterest. "Nothing. Just curious to see how far you've gone."

"Bullshit. You've always laughed at my needle wizardry since I started, and now you're suddenly curious?"

"It's called needle wizardry now? What happened to thread alchemy? That didn't last long."

"My sewing, my labels, sonny. So what's the deal?" Grandma's tightly puckered face—usually an indication of extreme irritation—loosened into a look of geriatric shock. "Oh, my hairy balls! Don't tell me you've seen him!"

Quinn could only stare at her in speechless amazement at first so that for several seconds, both merely gaped at each other over their half-eaten breakfast from opposite ends of the table.

"Grandma—what do you know?"

"What Bethany told me."

Quinn pinched his mouth and narrowed his eyes at her. "This conversation's going to take all day if I have to keep pushing you into saying more, Grandma. And remember it's my day off from work. I ain't going anywhere. Now spill."

Grandma set her coffee down and pushed the mug aside, so she could lean forward and glower magnificently at Quinn. She even rested both of her arms on the table, her fingers locking.

"The poor girl's dead, firstly. When she communicates with me, I mostly get images in my head—like memories or maybe stuff she projects into the future." She paused, her face puckering again. "Do dead people see into the future like Nostradamus? Is that something like necrophilia?"

"Necromancy. And I don't know. I'm kind of not dead."

"Anyway, that's how I get information from her."

"I thought you two have some creepy-ass girls' night out sort of deal and gossip away whenever she comes back to haunt the place."

Grandma clucked and shook her head. "Girls' night out," she grumbled. "Jesus, kid. If you were straight, you'd be a virgin."

"Grandma, I'm gay, and I'm *still* a virgin."

"The hell? Don't you bring shame to this family now!"

"I can't help it if other gay guys prank me with promises of a date, can I?"

That settled her down a little. "Those little bastards. You should've told me who they were, Quinn. I'd have gone out there and ripped their balls out with my teeth for hurting my grandson the way they did."

"You still have teeth?"

"Don't hate. False teeth are bomb proof nowadays. Mine can shred soft, hanging parts with one chomp if I'm pushed into defending an innocent boy's honor."

Quinn, his face burning, squirmed in his chair. "Can—can we go back to Bethany, please?"

"The girl's dead."

"Grandma!"

"I know, I know. I was just trolling you. Lighten up, kid, or you'll die of old age at twenty-five."

"I'm twenty-one!"

"Same difference." Grandma snorted and pulled her coffee mug back for a sip. "I get broken sentences from her whenever she does what ghosts do and suck up enough energy to be able to manifest or communicate. You know—paranormal mojo and all that."

Quinn nodded, relief washing over him now that the rickety conversation was finally moving forward. It took a great deal of effort, however, fighting off horrifying images of his grandmother ripping heartless gay men's dicks and balls with her dentures and going about the bloody deed like a pit bull. He took another bite of his pastry and waited.

"But for the most part, I just get stuff from her in my head. Pictures and feelings—mostly feelings that sort of turn into images when I connect with it in that psychic kind of way. That poor thing—gone too soon. Never had a happy life other than her having a baby."

Quinn nearly choked on his breakfast but managed to keep his cool. "Baby, huh? Did she ever say anything about that baby?"

"Other than she loved him. Still does, really. She cries a lot, poor kid—I mean, when she's verbal and when she feeds my brain with pictures." Grandma sighed and shook her head. She dropped her gaze to her coffee. "She wants him back, I think. Don't know what that means, but she does."

"Did she give you any idea how she lost her baby?"

Grandma was quiet for a moment, her attention suddenly drawn to the side of the room—more specifically, the wall shared by the two houses. "A prayer or something? Was that it? Christ, I can't remember. I do know it was shown to me a while back, and I was able to sew it. We have to go and look at what's there."

Quinn frowned. "Prayer? She said a prayer?"

"Not like a *prayer*-prayer, but more like a call. You know, a summons."

Quinn's skin crawled, and he grimaced. "You're saying she was a witch?"

"Can't say for sure. All I know is that she loved her baby so much she mojo-called someone or something to keep the baby safe when shit hit the fan. And that's it."

"Mojo-called," Quinn muttered. "You learn something new every day."

"I can tell you're snarking about me under your breath, mister."

Quinn sighed. "Do you think you can get her to talk more about her baby and what happened to him? Maybe you can get an idea of how she wants to get her son back."

"I don't have to. You can ask her yourself. She's standing right behind you."

Quinn howled, jumped, knocked his chair down, and bolted to his grandmother's side. Bug-eyed, glasses askew, his lungs and heart threatening to explode through his mouth, he stared at the other end of the table where his half-finished breakfast lay in a not-very-tempting mess. He'd somehow managed to flip his plate over, littering the table with crumbs and chunks of pastry. At least his tea remained intact. Other than the mess and the missing chair, his end of the table looked as cheerful as could be, with the bright sunlight's slanted beams spilling into the dining room and bestowing a certain innocent country charm to the scene.

"Jesus fucking Henry Christ," Grandma barked. "What were you trying to do, kid? Give me a heart attack? Are you gay virgins always this melodramatic when someone kids around?"

She took a long, loud sip of her coffee with visibly trembling hands.

# Chapter 10

Quinn watched in horrified fascination as Grandma gingerly—even reverently—unfolded her never-ending tapestry on the living room floor.

"Jesus, Grandma."

"Right? Okay, be careful. I think it's somewhere in this area." She paused, scowling thoughtfully as she inspected the patterns on the section currently exposed to scrutiny. "All right, maybe not. I guess I sewed it earlier on."

"Have you actually tried measuring this thing?"

Grandma snorted, her focus never wavering. Like an archeologist who'd struck gold at a dig and was now laying out every irreplaceable prize for critical assessment, she unfolded, examined carefully, and then refolded with amazing care and precision when she decided it wasn't the right place for her to stop. The living room was small, forcing her to topple headlong into obsessive-compulsive territory of unfolding and re-folding in her search for the pattern Quinn had asked for.

"Measure this masterpiece? Are you nuts? There's no way anyone in their right mind can put a number on this thing."

Other than the erratic spikes and dips of his grandmother's saving account, apparently, Quinn thought, wincing. He sat on the floor, cross-legged, on the other side of the tapestry, so he could help with the long and tedious process of finding the pattern he wanted to study. Of course, now that Grandma's supernaturally driven mania was fully laid bare, Quinn felt the initial stirrings of regret for pushing the issue.

Grandma paused all of a sudden. "What was your question again?"

Now would be the perfect time for Quinn to pretend amnesia and simply leg it, but his conscience reared up and forced the words out of him before he realized what he was doing. He really couldn't help it—not with Keaton's pleading features insinuating themselves into Quinn's mind.

"I wanted to see how she mojo-called creepy creatures to come and save her baby."

"Now it's my turn to ask," Grandma said, glancing up and leveling him with a narrow-eyed stare. "What do you know? You don't just bug me with questions from out of the blue and suddenly get all interested in my work."

Fair enough. In another moment, Quinn filled her in on what he'd learned from his research. That, of course, also meant he needed to talk about the sudden face-to-face with Keaton. Grandma listened closely to every word, her wrinkled face a masterpiece in twenty different human emotions all fighting to be clearly expressed in the shortest possible amount of time. More than once, Quinn's rambling account faltered and almost faded into fascinated silence as Grandma's myriad of human expressions distracted him enough to threaten a full derailment of his foray into amateur sleuthing.

"Holy mother of hell," Grandma breathed once he finished. "And there I was, all that time thinking it was such a cute idea to listen to Bethany when she asked me to send you to bed by ten. Made me think of you as that tiny little bundle of slimy-sticky spit-and-sugar joy from so long ago. I didn't realize it was because you'd likely be seeing this Keaton boy in the mirror at around that time."

"You're making her sound like a matchmaker."

"Well, isn't she? It does sound cute, though, doesn't it?" Then Grandma paused in what she was doing, shuffled forward on her hands and knees in order to reach across the fabric to pinch one of Quinn's cheek with a gurgling squee. "Aww, isn't that just adorable? My sweet little grandson's being set up with another boy by a dead girl."

"Sure, Grandma. Ow. *Ow.*"

"I've got a good feeling about this, but he'd better treat you right, or I'm coming after him. And I don't care if it means breaking the mirror and earning us seven years of bad luck. No one, but *no one,* breaks my little baby boy's heart again. I'm putting the world on notice."

Quinn alternately nodded and shook his head—the former in agreement, the latter in disbelief. Now that the cat was out of the bag, he did feel a great deal lighter and easier in his mind. When he saw a clear shift in Grandma's mood from shock to determination, he knew he now had an advantage in this situation, whatever that advantage might be.

Moral support? Yes, that was it.

Grandma had listened without judgment, and she'd easily taken to Quinn's fantastical account just as easily and smoothly as she'd taken to her strange friendship with a dead woman. All that gooey cooing over Bethany's matchmaking notwithstanding, of course...

"All right, then," she said, slapping her hands together and rubbing them with a delighted cackle. "Let's see how we can save your boyfriend, eh?"

"He's not my boyfriend. We just met, he might be a total jerk, or he might actually be cursed with dark fairy magic."

"Oh, please. You said he called you beautiful and wanted to kiss you."

Quinn swallowed, his face on fire now. "Yeah, I kind of regret telling you all that. Grandma, he might be a killer gnome disguised as James Steerforth." At his grandmother's quizzical frown, Quinn waved a dismissive hand. "Nothing. Just a fictional character I've been fantasizing about in the most sexually pathetic way possible."

"Sweetheart, I appreciate your honesty, but that was information I didn't ask for and didn't deserve to hear."

"Whatever, Grandma. It was therapeutic getting that off my chest, at least. Now can we please look into Keaton's situation?"

"Yep, sure. Works for me. Now here," she replied, turning her attention back to her tapestry and pointing at a section of the part she'd just unfolded. "I think this shows you what happened with the mojo-calling and all that."

Quinn leaned close and observed the patterns.

The section they were now studying showed the moment before and during Bethany's death. As with the rest of the patterns Grandma had sewn, these ones were quite crude in terms of shapes and details. Because Grandma never used a pencil to initially lay out the patterns, the limitations of the needle and thread hampered clarity, but Quinn was quite impressed all the same.

Only key moments of the tragedy were captured in thread, and they all looked like stills from a movie. A preschooler's cartoon movie, perhaps, but a movie all the same.

There was Bethany—as Quinn interpreted the nearly shapeless figure—cradling her baby and facing a full-length mirror. Judging from the way a nearby window was placed in relation to the mirror, it was safe to say that the moment took place in the attic room.

The next scene showed a second figure—Bethany's husband, it looked like—making an entrance with arms raised and fists aimed at her. She still held the baby close, her hunched figure indicating a terrified, defensive posture as she desperately protected her child from his father's rage. Then she was falling down the stairs in the next scene, the figure of her husband at the top, and he appeared to be flailing and cowering before another figure—one that seemed to push its upper body out of a rectangular frame on the wall. The newest figure's arms were outstretched, and a tiny bundle rested on the figure's hands.

The baby, Quinn thought, being saved from certain death by a creature—whatever it might be—that had been summoned for help. The rectangular frame could only mean a mirror, very much like the mirror now hanging on the wall by the stairs. It stood to reason that mirrors were the otherworld's one of many different doorways to the world of mortals.

"Okay," Quinn said after a long moment's silence. "These pretty much tie in to what we already know. But how do we find out the summoning spell or prayer Bethany used? I think that ought to be our key to helping Keaton get out of the creepy world he's in."

Grandma shook her head as she tried to unfold the rest of the tapestry.

"Damn it," she breathed. "This is the end of the line. Or the beginning of the whole sordid drama, anyway. There's nothing here that can tell us how Bethany did it." She looked up, worry darkening her features. "Now what do we do?"

Quinn considered for a moment. "Do you think you can get Bethany to communicate with you again? Or is it usually pretty random?"

"It's random, but I can also tell when she's here."

Quinn couldn't help the unease returning and making his hair stand on end. He'd never had any close encounters with ghosts, and while he hoped he never would, he also knew it was only a matter of time in this case. Especially since he seemed to be marked for a highly unusual task, which meant there was simply no way around the inevitable haunting.

He thought about his mother and her not-quite-fully-tapped psychic abilities. She'd been receptive to Bethany's plea for help, and that had likely been the deal-breaker where all the other house-hunters were concerned. And it had taken Fate seven years for the Geiger family to cross paths with Destiny. Quinn's mother had been the only one to show up with some ability to see the other side, allowing Bethany to perhaps use any kind of paranormal sympathetic ability Mrs. Geiger had in order to root herself firmly into this half of the duplex.

Over the years—seven times two in this instance—that physical and spiritual regeneration took place, preparing Quinn as he matured for this task. Those regenerative years could also be for Bethany, who waited and watched from her world, perhaps drawing strength and hope from Quinn's develop- ment. Those regenerative years could also be for Keaton, who seemed to live in a perpetual state of enchantment that was also in danger of threatening his sur- vival if his thinness was something to go by. Every little detail seemed to be as equally important as the others, and mulling over things like this could easily drive a man insane, but Quinn knew better than to let himself be swept away so easily.

He helped Grandma fold the remaining tapestry before helping her to her feet as well.

"Could you try to communicate with her?" he asked, hoping she could read the earnestness in his face and his tone. "I'll go and find out what I can about summoning spells."

He led her to the couch and gently sat her down, her tapestry resting on her lap and her giant sewing basket sitting on the floor by her feet. She regarded him dubiously but didn't resist his somewhat distracted fussing.

"Where are you going to go? The Institute of Arcane Studies is only open to sorcerers, isn't it?"

"Yeah, I know, but I'll check with Edwin first and see if he knows anyone."

"Oof. Christ, he really can't get rid of you, can he?"

Quinn was now patting his jeans for his wallet, and once satisfied, he marched over to the coffee table, where he'd tossed his keys and his hoodie.

"No, he can't." Quinn shrugged on his hoodie and grinned at Grandma. "At this point he's pretty much learned the hard way that shit happens when you hire me."

"Make sure that's not on your résumé, okay? We can't depend on my social security checks alone to survive in this crazy-expensive state. And be careful, kiddo—you know there's a damn good reason why only real, honest-to-good- ness, badass sorcerers can use magic."

Quinn caught the worry in her voice thought she still put on her usual Gruff Grandma face, and he nodded, smiling. "I will," he said. "I promise."

"Oh, and if you're going to see Edwin, do you think you can bug him for a recipe for *pancit*? I don't know if it's possible for someone my age to get preg- nant again, but I've been really craving for that stuff on and off for a while now. I just haven't asked you about it."

Quinn made the mistake of considering what she'd just said and immediately regretted it. Stomach churning, he bleated, "Not-Quite-Immaculate Conception much, Grandma?"

"Right? Pretty crazy and not to mention pretty gross, as you kids say nowadays."

# Chapter 11

"Okay, so why're we here again?"

"A year of nightmare material for you and absolute, unshakable moral support for me."

"Fuck you, Quinn."

Quinn glanced over his shoulder to level a scowling Edwin with a thousand-watt grin. "See that? I didn't even flinch when you cussed me out. That's what I meant when I said 'absolute' and 'unshakable.'"

Edwin rolled his eyes and directed his scowl everywhere else, hands on his hips. "As usual, you're not making a whole lot of sense, but whatever."

He walked cautiously toward a particularly gothic-looking collection of vines breaking out of the ruined floor and creeping up the nearest wall. Quinn thought they looked like a dozen skeletal arms and hands reaching out vainly for something in the living world.

"I gave you the recipe for *pancit*. Guess that wasn't enough to get rid of your ass."

Quinn ignored him, his attention having been hooked by the dusty and broken mirror hanging beyond reach on the wall, where the stairs had been. He'd been mentally mapping out his own home and determining whether or not the placement of furniture and even wall decorations perfectly mirrored those in the doomed structure. A chill rippled up and down his arms as he pondered because the more he compared things in his head, the more convinced he was that his home was the literal twin of this one.

"You can't reach that. The stair's gone—well, kind of gone," Edwin's voice cut through the uneasy muddle of thoughts in Quinn's head.

"I wish I could, though."

"Dude, I'm sure there's a reason why this place is now something like a pretty freaky fairy tale house. I can definitely feel the death vibes ever since I walked through that door, but it's like I'm not scared. Know what I mean? It's just—creepy. I mean—yeah, death up the wazoo, but at the same time, just creepy."

Like being in another world, Quinn couldn't help but append. Or at least be standing in the middle of a dark hybrid of a home, one that straddled two completely different worlds. He wondered if this was something akin to being in the outskirts of an invisible world or kingdom, considering how seamless the melding of natural and supernatural elements was whenever he ventured inside this ruined shell.

He took a few steps away, his gaze moving to other parts of the upper floors as he tried to think back to what he'd seen in his grandmother's tapestry. When he realized Edwin had gone unnaturally silent, he looked at his friend and found him staring long and hard at the ruined stairway.

"Edwin, what're you doing?" he asked.

"Counting—well, more like mentally calculating how many steps were made going up to the second floor." Edwin made a distracted gesture with a vague wave of a hand. "I'm using estimated measurements based on the steps that're still intact. You know, nerdy math stuff."

"Um—okay."

"The stairs ended with *mata* if my calculations are right." Edwin looked at Quinn and jerked his head at the ruined stairs. "If my calculations are spot on, the stairs ended with death. Or *mata*. It's a common superstition in the Philippines when it comes to house-building. Each step on the stairs means something, and the saying goes: *oro, plata, mata*. Gold, silver, death. Technically, you should never end with *mata,* or it's like cursing your house with a shit ton of bad luck while it's standing."

Quinn pursed his lips. "I don't think the architects of the duplex knew anything about Filipino superstition, dude. They just designed the stairs to, you know, let people move from the first floor to the second floor."

Edwin pointed at the mirror as though Quinn hadn't said anything remotely rational. "That mirror up there? It's in line with a step that would also be *mata.*"

"Maybe it's coincidence?"

"Maybe it's not?"

Quinn raised both hands as his brain threatened to walk off its job and squeeze out of his ears in protest. "Okay, so are you saying we need to consult with Filipino sorcerers for this? Do you think one of your homies might be able to help Keaton get back to us?"

"I don't know. Until we find out who designed and built this place, we're kind of stuck asking whoever's willing to give us the time of the day, right?" Edwin shrugged, a sheepish little smile playing up his face. "But I've got connections if you're interested. My brother's best buddies with a couple of Filipino sorcerers."

"Okay, that'll be cool. I can tackle my homies at the same time."

Quinn fell silent as he considered the stairs and did his own mental counting. "That doesn't make any sense. If in your culture, the stairs should end with gold, which would be one, four, seven, eleven, and thirteen, it's like you guarantee yourself good luck with the number thirteen."

"Well—who says superstitions make any sense? I'm not blind, and I've been whacking off since I figured out how to party with Mr. Happy."

"Goddamnit, boss. Not cool."

Edwin shrugged. "You drag my ass over here? You pay the piper."

"I'd rather get a raise, thank you very much." Quinn sighed and spared a glance at the mirror. "I wonder if anyone knew this place was going to be built on some kind of border between this world and the otherworld."

"Well—considering we're not under attack by fairies, ghouls, vampires, and monster angel statues that come to life, it's pretty safe to say it wasn't done on purpose. Like this duplex being here was just nothing but pure dumb luck. And if Keaton's claims are anything to go by, it looks like we're not in any real danger from whoever he's hanging out with."

"Yeah, maybe they think we're dumb and boring if they're even aware our world exists next to theirs. Best to let them keep thinking that, so they'll stay the hell away from ours. Though—I remember him saying they used to be from our world or something like that."

"True, but your boyfriend's also kind of out there in the mental department. You did say he's like a little rambly and distracted—like he's under a spell. He could be saying a bunch of stuff that doesn't really mean anything."

"I know. Sucks, but I know."

Quinn led the way out—not that it was a difficult thing to do, considering they kept their sleuthing in the general area of the damaged stairwell—his mind racing. He hated to admit it, but he wouldn't even know where to begin when it came to asking around for help from sorcerers. Did those people even charge consultation fees, let alone actual sorcery work? How much would a custom spell cost if things came down to that in getting Keaton back?

"What about your mirror?" Edwin prodded once they were outside again, reveling in the comfort of the bright morning sun. "If we checked out the alter ego that's hanging in your house, would it tell us something?"

"Not if you mojo the hell out of it," Quinn replied, sighing. "I've stood in front of that thing so many times now, and nothing's happened. If anything, I've only had that one incident before—like a sighting of Keaton, I'm sure now—and it was totally a second or two seconds, tops. Everything else happened upstairs in my attic room."

Which meant that, when the neighboring house was still intact, Bethany might have used it perhaps to activate her summoning spell. She might have tried to open a door in a desperate bid to save herself and her baby, but Quinn wondered if she was simply too slow in engaging forces from the otherworld to get the job done correctly. She was a battered woman, she was at her wits' end, and she wasn't a sorcerer. If she'd somehow learned about summoning spells from somewhere, she wouldn't have been able to pull it off successfully or effectively.

His thoughts wandered back to fairies and the very strong possibility of Glass-Dreams being a world of the wee folk. Or not-so-wee folk according to some lore. Two mirror worlds, perhaps, with Glass-Dreams steeped in so much magic that it had, somehow, managed to keep a human baby alive, even allow it to grow and flourish and be educated in languages and other things. Keaton would refer to them as "people" since they'd be his only real contact with other beings who came very close to ordinary mortals in physiology. It really shouldn't come as a surprise if his exposure to all things related to fairies would affect his perception of who and what they were.

Bethany managing to reach out to a being from a darker world with a summoning spell certainly made the fairy angle even more plausible. What other creature in folklore and legend was capable of pulling off such a miracle? And judging from Keaton's bizarre, dreamy state and mildly distracted conversation, it was clear to Quinn that the young man was under some dark spell. So much so, in fact, that Keaton also appeared to be gradually wasting away in Glass-Dreams if his pallid complexion and alarmingly thin figure were anything to go by.

Quinn had very little knowledge of the fairy world and of fairies, specifically, despite his current work. All he knew about them was that they were terribly unpredictable creatures, prone to displays of gratitude and, conversely, acts of petty revenge. And while it was true that poor Bethany's pleas had been answered, at what cost did she see her dearest wish granted—besides her life, that is? Keaton was safe, and by all appearances, he was well cared for and even educated in the ways of mortals. But was he trapped in Glass-Dreams forever? Or was there an expiration date to the spell Bethany had used in her desperation? Was that why these odd events had been happening with greater and greater frequency?

Keaton's time must be running out. Quinn swallowed at the thought. It was the only logical explanation he could think of, particularly when Grandma claimed that Bethany had been grieving and wanting her child back.

In another moment Quinn was safely buckled inside Edwin's car, and they were puttering through the crowded streets of Dolores toward Tess's bakery. Her dream business was located in an old live-and-work strip just off Dolores's main boulevard, and she'd claimed a pair of "cute gay men" lived together in the apartment directly above her work. One of them, she'd also said, was a practicing sorcerer who'd saved the life of his boyfriend a couple or more years ago, and it was simply too bad she was married and that they weren't into bisexual threesomes.

"She really said that?" Quinn asked, blinking owlishly at Edwin, whose tightly screwed features got worse and worse as he recounted Tess's swoony descriptions of the happy—and, apparently, hot—gay couple. "Really? No shit?"

"No shit. Well—at least they're gay, and she can only look and drool. No real chance of her running off with them one day."

"They buy stuff from her bakery a lot?"

"Probably. They live upstairs, so it'd be stupid for them not to take advantage. Most likely if she decides to give them fangirl discounts, and she'd better fucking not."

Quinn couldn't help his grin, but he at least took care to turn his face away and pretend interest in the sights and sounds of downtown Dolores. He was definitely taking a big risk, doing this cold call thing and consulting someone he'd never met before. Tess's lust-filled accounts of the pair would make for questionable recommendations as far as Quinn was concerned, but if Keaton was in any real danger, scruples be damned. He didn't even know if either of the pair would be home when they stopped by, and he almost laughed at himself for being a complete and hopeless idiot.

"You know, I've heard from my brother's friends that the internet's really turning magic into a real shit show," Edwin piped up after a moment's silence. He paused at a stop sign, signaled a turn, and took the next right. "All kinds of crazy stuff gets put up online, and that includes illegal magic—I don't know—tools, merchandise, spells, and all that."

"You think that Bethany might've gotten her summoning spell that way?"

"I wouldn't be surprised if she did. And that'll only make it even harder for us to track the source down."

Quinn chewed his lip as he mulled that over. "Well—it's really too late now at this point. What's more important is figuring out exactly what kind of world Glass-Dreams is and how we can get Keaton out of there."

They finally stopped before a row of quaint shops that ran the gamut from hand-woven and hand-dyed yarn to exotic teas and herbs. The street itself looked like something out of a time capsule, with live-and-work spaces clustered together in a weathered and antiquated show of discolored brick, decorated glass, and hanging signs on scroll brackets. Here and there, wooden benches flanked by potted plants were set against blank walls separating adjoining shops.

Edwin and Quinn's parking spot was a prime one, located directly in front of Tess's bakery. Instinctively, Quinn glanced up and searched the windows directly above it. He thought he saw a face peering down from one, dark eyes locking gazes with his. And in another second, the face was gone.

# Chapter 12

Quinn looked at Edwin, who sat on an armchair perpendicular to the sofa he'd planted himself on. His friend's face had reached full Puckered Grandma levels, and Quinn actually felt a touch worried.

"Hey," he whispered as he leaned toward his friend. "You know what they say about a bad wind blowing and turning that weird-ass look on your face into a permanent one."

"That Efrain dude's a lot hotter than I expected," Edwin muttered. His eyes, narrowed to near slits, were the only parts of his body that showed any life as they tracked the movements of their host. The young man was currently puttering around the small kitchen and getting refreshments ready while blissfully unaware of the animosity he was causing.

That Efrain Thorley, sorcerer-hunter extraordinaire, was handsome, smart, and friendly only added to poor Edwin's internal drama of boiling jealousy. When Quinn reminded him of Efrain's homosexuality, things only seemed to get worse. Instead of reassurance, a withering irritation appeared to set in with Edwin hissing an admission that Efrain being gay only made him even more appealing to women because they adored gorgeous, untouchable men. Naturally.

Quinn sighed, eyeing him dully. "Hate to break this to you, but straight people sure have some pretty serious issues."

"Don't I know that."

Efrain finally walked out of the kitchen toward them, moving so smoothly and so easily that even Quinn felt the initial stirrings of jealousy toward Efrain's live-in boyfriend, who was currently at work. His earlier thorough observation of the small apartment only added to the angst of his own inadequacies. Little details here and there, random objects normally overlooked or dismissed as inconsequential, quietly spoke of a relationship that was quite young still yet was full of comfort and domestic ease.

On the coffee table sat a small glass jar half-filled with smooth, black stones, among which was tucked a handwritten "Sparrow Beach: Leander's birthday no. 24" on a torn piece of paper. The note itself had about it a quality of an afterthought and a hastily made choice, at that. Quinn didn't know why he immediately jumped on that notion, but he simply couldn't help it. There was something extremely special and wonderfully innocent about the note itself that made him give it more thought than he normally would have.

A bundle of dried roses carefully tied with a gauzy blue ribbon lay on a side table. There was something about the way the flowers were set on what one would consider a random surface that spoke of incredible care and affection. Indeed, the mere sight of dried flowers that would have long been thrown in the garbage bin revealed another rich facet of the bond between Efrain and Leander.

A cheap, avocado-colored mug held two pairs of chopsticks elaborately decorated with magic symbols in fine gold paint. The mug and its pretty contents sat on what was probably a place of honor on a nearby shelf. Quinn took note of the fact that the two pairs of chopsticks were also linked to each other by the presence of a thin and silky red ribbon looped around each set. He remembered reading about the Chinese lore of the red thread of fate when he was still in college, and he'd absolutely adored the idea. And now there it was, just a few feet away from him, a shockingly simple representation of an unbreakable connection between soulmates.

Quinn could only read all of these little details as quiet representations of an unassuming but strong bond of love that might have been forged from a shared past replete with shadows and fear, possibly danger, given Efrain's calling. He wondered about himself—more notably his future self and whatever chances of happiness might be in store for him. If Keaton, who'd never met a fellow mortal till now, seemed to be Quinn's single hope for a happy romance, things were definitely not looking all that well.

"I guess I really should go out more," he murmured grudgingly.

Then he reminded himself of Matt and the others who'd heartlessly toyed with his hopes, and he immediately nixed the half-hearted self-criticism.

"Me and Tess have been saying the same thing since I hired you."

"Shut up, Edwin. Quit listening in on my self-hating monologues."

Efrain reached the living room at that moment, bearing a tray of sliced rolls and coffee. "Here you go. Help yourselves. I got these from the bakery downstairs. The staff there are always super sweet and always force me and Leander to take some extra goodies home at the end of the day."

"Uh—did they give you a steep discount for these?" Edwin demanded.

"Nope. Just the usual end-of-the-day discount of fifty percent."

Edwin grunted in answer, which, apparently, meant he was fine with the half off special. Quinn sensed some of the black cloud of jealousy come out of him as though his body had just halfway purged itself of toxins with a particularly wretched fart.

"Go on, dig in," Efrain piped up, looking rather pleased with his presentation. "It's really good."

Never ones to look a gift horse in the mouth, Quinn and Edwin dove in with great alacrity. That said, Quinn suspected Edwin snatched a particularly large slice of mocha roll to shove into his mouth to keep himself from blurting out potentially rude things to their host about being a virtual gay sex god to adoring straight women everywhere. Efrain, in the meantime, seated himself in a chair he'd brought from the tiny dining room. He picked up the folder of printouts Quinn had brought and lost himself in a quick skim of their contents. Quinn and Edwin had already given him the general run-down of the strange mystery surrounding Keaton's situation after their initial introductions.

"So your question involves the summoning spell that'd been used," Efrain said at length. "And whether or not this Glass-Dreams place is the world of fairy."

"Um—before we go on, how much do you charge for consultations?" Quinn asked with a painfully self-conscious raise of a hand. "Because this is kind of a spur-of-the-moment thing for us."

Efrain blinked, looking genuinely startled. "Well, I don't charge anything. In fact, you guys are my first ever consultation since I'm not really into sorcery for hire, in a sense. I mean, I hunt and all that, but it's a calling, and I was recently hired to be a part of the faculty at the Institute of Arcane Studies as a part-time lecturer. I also still work part-time at a custom frame shop to help my uncle out and make sure my bills are paid. I don't mind, really, just talking and helping you figure things out. It'll be good for the old brain cells."

He smiled and poked the side of his head with a finger.

"Okay, cool. Thanks." Quinn exchanged looks with Edwin, who nodded. "So, yeah—summoning spell. We think that whatever deal Bethany might have made with fairies has some kind of time limit. And that Keaton needs to be taken back from that world before—I don't know—he's trapped there forever."

Efrain nodded and stayed quiet for another moment, his gaze fixed on the printouts though his mind was obviously elsewhere.

"To be honest with you, I don't know what kind of summoning spell Bethany might've used," he said, looking up with a slight frown. "If that was what it was, though I really doubt it."

"But—you didn't study that in sorcery academy or anything?" Quinn stammered. He blushed when a bemused half-smile replaced Efrain's frown. "Sorry. I don't know what kind of school sorcerers went to to get all totally badass with magic and stuff. Other than, you know, the Institute of Arcane Studies, which, I guess, is really a sorcery academy, isn't it? Uh..."

"Dude, stop," Edwin muttered with a pointed side-eye.

Efrain just shook his head, his smile broadening. "It's okay. Now—this Glass-Dreams. It sounds like a fairy world, but this is Dolores City, not Ireland or Scotland or any place in Europe, Africa, or Asia with a long history and tradition of fairy legends and so on. Dolores is—well, it's a city of mourning. Loss."

And, he continued, any magic local to the city was defined by grief—or shadowed by it. The city's past was certainly the stuff of legend, with no one fully confirming the story of Dolores's founding. Facts long obscured by whispered rumors had evolved, though, and a common thread had emerged over time: the legend of La Llorona. Or something mirroring it, anyway, in the way loss, guilt, grief, and death shrouded the old, old tale of the weeping woman. Because of the rise of technology and the internet, information easily got muddied further, with too many voices online claiming authority over one thing or another. But many, sorcerers and ordinary residents alike, knew too well just how the dark nature of Dolores affected and shaped otherworldly elements that found their way into people's lives now and then. It was almost like being in a surreal hybrid of a bustling city and a necropolis, with the dead still exerting a potent influence over the living.

And with that said, Efrain went on to explain what sort of world Glass-Dreams would most likely be.

"I'd say it's something like one of those popular theories about what kind of spirits or beings fairies are in Europe," he said. "The more I think about it, the more I'm convinced that Glass-Dreams is basically a world inhabited by souls of the dead that somehow got detached from both this world and the next."

"You mean like limbo?" Edwin piped up, and Efrain nodded.

"So they're going around thinking they're actually alive, and the world they live in has some kind of ghost mojo thing?" Quinn prodded, blinking in some confusion.

Efrain inclined his head thoughtfully. "It's safe to say that their world's shaped by centuries of souls—well, their willpower, anyway, or whatever psychic and emotional ties they've kept with them in death. Like residual essences from their mortal lives that never got to be purged completely when they died. Past beliefs, values, passions, etc., are still there, probably as nothing more than echoes or shadows. Their will to live is strong enough to trap them in a world of weird magic. When did this world start? I don't know. It's old, that's for sure, or it wouldn't be as developed as the way Quinn described it. Or the way you've seen it, with the attic room and even Keaton's clothes."

"Don't you usually hunt these ghosts, though?" Quinn asked.

Efrain's features darkened a little, as though he were now forced to think of less academic and more painful things. "No. the ghosts I hunt wander around Dolores. None of them are confined to a world that pretty much keeps them away from the rest of us. They're a completely different breed, in a sense."

"So—let me get this straight." Edwin paused to sip his coffee. "When people die—at least here in Dolores—they either go into the light, so to speak, or they get sucked into Glass-Dreams somehow, or they haunt the city and get exorcised by sorcerer-hunters like you."

"That's the theory," Efrain replied as he set the folder back on the coffee table. "There might be other ways a soul gets trapped, but no one's aware of it yet. Like an invisible door or portal that's somewhere out there, and every now and then, the soul of a recently deceased person goes through it. Most likely because of certain residual essences that might act like a key, which is why most souls move on, but some get stuck in this limbo. Or maybe the living have something to do with it. There are some, you know, who actively try to bring the dead back because—because they can't accept loss, and they'll do anything for that second chance." He paused, another shadow momentarily darkening his features. "As an example—I've also seen a case in which a soul got trapped as punishment for breaking a magical contract. It does happen, unfortunately."

He didn't bother to elaborate on that, but Quinn suspected it must have been an incident Efrain had had an unsettling experience with. He sat back and considered, his gaze straying to the folder.

"So how do we figure out how to get Keaton out? If what you're saying is true about the people surrounding him—which is just beyond messed up, by the way—then it's safe to say there's no real summoning spell to get them to pay attention to us?"

"This is how I'm interpreting Bethany's story. She lived with an abusive husband, and the only thing that brought her happiness was her baby," Efrain said. "The duplex your family live in is somehow the thinnest part of the veil separating Glass-Dreams from this world. I'm guessing her trauma—the constant elevated levels of anger and sadness in her home—made contact with the others possible. If anything, her being able to cry for help and have someone from Glass-Dreams respond must have meant that she was only step away from death."

Edwin and Quinn were silent for a moment, with each of them squirming in their seats as they pondered what they'd learned. Quinn had never been this unnerved by a semi-social visit before.

"I guess it makes sense," he said at length. "I mean—I've heard of people having weird experiences right before they died all of a sudden—like they were marked for death or destined to die, and that made them sort of vulnerable to hauntings or something."

Beside him, Edwin sighed loudly as he stared at his empty dessert plate. "I really want to hug the shit out of my cats right now. Life kind of demands it."

# Chapter 13

Grandma remained silent for a moment after Quinn gave her the lowdown on the nature of Glass-Dreams.

"Well, damn," she breathed, shaking her head. "That poor girl. So what now, kiddo?"

Quinn shrugged and scratched his head helplessly. "Not really sure, to be honest. By the way, have you been feeling like you're at death's door lately? Heard the grim reaper's creepy voice calling out to you before you fall asleep? I think the very, very last moment before you pass out is when you're most vulnerable to that stuff."

Grandma stared at him in what could only be incredulous silence before outrage set in. She pulled herself up to her full, imposing height of five feet and leveled Quinn with a withering scowl.

"What, can't wait for me to kick the bucket so you can make off with your inheritance, eh? Well, tough shit, buddy, because I've got no plans of croaking yet."

"Grandma, whatever inheritance money used to be there has gone to your thread alchemy habit. I was just wondering if what Efrain said about how Bethany got to communicate with Glass-Dreams is true or not."

"That's no comfort. It means the only way for that to be proven is for one of us to be marked for death, and it sure ain't going to be me." Grandma punctuated her retort with a very porcine snort.

"Don't give me that look. I'm too young to go yet."

"Oh? Tell that to Bethany."

"She was killed." Quinn eyed her narrowly. "Unless you're planning to off me anytime soon."

"I admit you make me want to commit grandchildicide sometimes, but I always remind myself you're still young and only need a good smack upside the head or even an occasional epic wedgie to keep you in line." With that, she marched over to Quinn, took hold of his face with both hands, and yanked him down to give him a kiss on the forehead. "Mwah! You know I wuv you, kiddo, and giving you epic wedgies hurt me more than they hurt you."

"Thanks. Love you, too, Grandma," he said once he was again upright, and the world had stopped spinning. He staggered toward the refrigerator to dig around for something to eat. "So how do you think I was able to see Keaton that time?"

"If the only way for the door to open was for death to be sniffing around, I'll say it'd have to be Bethany. I mean, neither of us is about to croak anytime soon—gruesome accidents not included—so it's only logical, isn't it? She's our link to the other side. I mean you did mention cold spots, and I might be ancient and out of touch with modern society to some extent, but I know cold spots usually mean ghosts. So there—Bethany equals door to other side. Ta-da!"

"With Glass-Dreams, it's more like not-quite-other-side."

"True, that."

Quinn pulled out a container of half-finished *leche* flan, which Edwin and Tess gave him the previous day. Taking a dessert plate, a cake knife, and a spoon from the cupboards and utensil drawers, he settled himself at the table. Grandma never cared for the flan—much to Quinn's greedy delight—and busied herself with coffee and a scone.

"Kind of makes you wish we had our own ghost-on-command thing going, doesn't it? Like some kind of supernatural switch that we can flick on and off."

"Jesus, kid. If you were a sorcerer, you'd be the kind who'd be hunted down and executed for crimes against the dead."

"I know, right?" Quinn shuddered, suddenly too aware he'd just weirded himself out over—himself. He wouldn't admit it openly, of course, but he used to think there was a particularly dark, anti-heroic charm in being a necromancer.

Grandma sighed and pondered her afternoon snack. "I'll see if I can get Bethany to communicate again and, you know, help us reach out to your boyfriend again."

Quinn grimaced. "I'm sure it takes a lot of energy for her to pull that off, and that means who knows when she'll be able to come to us next. Oh, and he's not my boyfriend."

"Not yet." Then shocker of shockers, Grandma winked at Quinn before giggling like a wrinkled tween girl.

* * * *

The rest of the afternoon passed relatively peacefully, though Quinn was sure the anticipation of Bethany's next haunting tainted the familiar, domestic ease with an undercurrent of mild dread and a generous helping of eeriness. Now and then, Quinn wondered—couldn't help but toy with the idea, that is—if knowledge had ruined something he'd at first shrugged off as quirkily magical. Indeed, Keaton's existence in what initially appeared to be a darkly enchanted world had given Quinn too many romanticized ideas about Keaton's world despite his awareness of the young man's tragic backstory.

With Efrain Thorley's help, the mystery of Keaton of Glass-Dreams had now taken an even darker turn, though no physical threat seemed to be there. Or at least from Quinn's interpretation of Efrain's theories, Keaton was only in danger of being trapped in the world of aimless souls. As of tea time, Keaton appeared to be safe from dismemberment, blood drainage, organ rearrangement, and every other variation of those.

But to be living all that time among souls of the dead, who apparently went about their days behaving as though they were absolutely clueless about the permanent absence of their physical bodies, let alone their previous lives...

And the possible threat to be trapped there forever should Quinn fail?

"Where the hell would his soul go?" Quinn muttered, glancing up from his book and giving the mirror on the stairs a nervous look. "Better yet, would he even know the difference if he dies there? Would he just wake up one day, totally dead, but still go around not even knowing he'd just left his physical body behind?"

He thinned his lips and shuddered as he forced his attention back to his book. Sitting on the sofa and facing the stairs with its ominous mirror wasn't doing his mind any favors, apparently. Too many reminders of a tragic past, an unsettling present, and a terrifyingly unknown future—plus the fact that both houses in the duplex were mirror images of each other down to furniture arrangement and even the placement of wall hangings like the mirror on the stairs.

The reminder of his home's furnishing arrangement gave him the creeps. To what extent were his parents' decisions to set this table there and that chair here dictated by influences from the world of the dead? Were they even aware of something unnatural other than the nagging belief that the house had cho-sen them, specifically, to live in it? There was no way he could call his father overseas and bother him with superstitious things. His mother had always been the one who'd been keenly aware of something else working under the surface of the material world. His father was the pragmatist and the businessman.

And if his home's furnishings echoed the placement of those in Bethany's former house, chances were Mrs. Geiger had been somehow "inspired" to make it so. The possibility of her going about the eerie twin-decorating without any conscious thought about why she made this choice or that was also quite high. And the more Quinn considered it, the surer he felt about his mother's latent psychic ability turning her into Bethany's desperately needed conduit between the world of the living and the dead.

She'd also allowed Bethany the chance to thin the veil between two worlds in a mad bid to save her poor son.

Quinn's unease spiked at another thought. He sat there, feeling like he was about to watch the horror of Bethany's death as though the event had been cap-tured on video and was now doomed to be replayed into infinity even if the event had taken place next door. He'd long known that some hauntings were believed to be psychic imprints of events, producing something like a feedback loop under certain environmental conditions. In this instance, the two hous-es and the worlds they contained had overlapped like two sides of one mirror merging into each other, perhaps irreversibly, and what should be haunting the adjoining ruins would likely be haunting Quinn's home.

"Okay, I've got to stop this. I'm seriously freaking myself out over stuff that I can't even prove."

From Grandma's bedroom came the familiar foghorn blast of a dozing se-nior. Grandma had miraculously passed out after a coffee-and-sugar binge, and Quinn wondered if being able to collapse into his bed after that kind of indul-gence for a nap was genetic. He'd certainly appreciate it if it were. Then again, Grandma wasn't the one obsessing over the Keaton dilemma and had no real incentive to prop her eyelids open while waiting for a dead woman's ghost to manifest in some way.

Bracing himself despite the awful sensation of goosebumps breaking out all over, Quinn cleared his throat and tried to focus on his task.

"Um—Bethany? It's me, Quinn. I'm sure you pretty much know me already since you and Grandma have been kind of communicating with each other for a while now."

Quinn spoke in as low a volume as he could manage without whispering. Despite the snores coming out of the open door to his grandmother's bedroom, the house remained silent, and Quinn hated it, the more he paid attention to it. And it was because the silence seemed abnormal.

From outside came the muted street noises, but none of them eased the tomb-like hollowness of his home. At first Quinn thought it was nothing more than the product of his imagination, but a pat answer always failed to convince. The silence felt different somehow, and he didn't like it. It, in effect, echoed the peculiar silence of the ruins next door, hinting at something—a yet unknown event—about to happen.

"Anyway," he continued, rallying his spirits, "I know what happened to you and Keaton. I'd like to help bring him back. I know you were the one who led me to the mirror upstairs."

He paused as his thoughts flew a little further back in time, and he looked up at the mirror on the stairs again. "I'm pretty sure now I caught a glimpse of Keaton in that mirror over there that one time, too. It was super quick, and for a while, I wasn't sure if I was just imagining things, but I know better now."

Quinn frowned and looked around the living room. Was it just him, or did the room temperature drop all of a sudden? He looked at the nearest window and saw bright sunlight still streaming through. There was no gathering storm outside, at least.

"I know it isn't good for me—for anyone—to call on someone who's dead and expect them to come. And I know I should help you cross over and be at peace forever."

The chill deepened, and Quinn hugged himself. Even in the afternoon hours, with the sun still up, the horrible feeling of having someone else in the room with him filled him with a creeping sort of terror. It was all he could do to recall Keaton's romantic, Victorian gentleman airs and manner to keep himself from having a full-on freakout.

"But in order for me to do that, I have to help you bring your son back. Can you—can you show me how?"

A voice—so soft, so low—whispered close by.

"Pray for me...pray for me..."

"I—I don't pray, but I swear I'll try my best to help you. For what it's worth, I'm really very sorry for what happened to you and Keaton. I can't imagine how things were back then for you, and I wish someone had helped you and your baby before it was too late."

The whispers died in a faint and drawn-out sigh, but the chill lingered, and it felt as though someone had just edged close and wrapped their arms around Quinn. Offering him comfort? Or seeking comfort instead? He sure couldn't tell, and despite the terror that had gripped him and was now rising steadily with every rapid pounding of his heart, he found that he couldn't move even if he wanted to. Perhaps this was the first step to helping poor Bethany some much-needed rest and closure after all those years—twenty-one, to be exact—of simply waiting for the right moment to nudge her chosen champion in the direction of a dark world.

Allowing himself to be held—if that was what Bethany was doing at the moment—by a woman who'd died knowing nothing but grief and pain would have to be the least he could do. He'd be her son by proxy even if only for a handful of seconds. He'd show her his determination not to cower in fear before the unknown. By not abandoning her, he'd prove to her that her faith in his mother and, in turn, in him wasn't in vain.

All the same, Quinn couldn't help a tiny, fearful whimper escape his tightly pinched mouth and the question of whether or not that was a wet spot growing in his jeans.

# Chapter 14

Quinn stood on the topmost step, eyeing his bedroom door warily. Bethany's visit had been too brief, the chill marking her presence gone in only a handful of seconds. Quinn wondered if it meant she simply had a difficult time drawing energy to herself in order to communicate in broken whispers with no clear message to give him. No instructions on how to proceed. All the same, however, something in his gut urged him to go to his room, and even more bewildering was the overriding need to leave a short note to his grandmother.

"I'm in my bedroom," it read. "B was just here. I'll see if she can help me find K."

It *was* a pretty silly, nonsensical thing to do, telling her where he'd be, and what was even sillier was the fact he felt a vague sense of dread when he wrote it. He was nervous, and that was all, he kept telling himself. He felt as though he'd been thrown into the deep end of the pool, and while nothing in his experiences so far warned him of going up against the kind of danger a seasoned sorcerer like Efrain Thorley faced day after day, he was still very much a novice in this. An ordinary young man with no real skill or talent in magic to boast of. One who'd less than zero experience in all things supernatural, most especially in a situation involving the extraction of a mortal from a dark dreamscape of aimless souls.

"Okay, okay. I can do this."

He swung the door open and strode inside with confidence, his gaze taking in his bedroom in a couple of sweeps. Nothing out of the ordinary to see, much to his dismay, but the quiet buzz of nervous energy turned into a compulsion to stay and wait. Quinn left his bedroom door ajar and walked over to his bed, hesitating for a second or two as he tried to clear his mind and open his senses to subtler hints of something unusual. Again there was nothing, but the muted dread that had been gnawing away at his mind was still there, still insistent, still feeding his sense of self-preservation with a wordless warning to be on the alert.

And sure enough, it happened the very second Quinn sat on the bed.

He sprang back up with a startled gasp. "Bethany? Keaton?" he called.

"Quinn?"

Wide-eyed and his heart lodging itself in his throat, Quinn turned toward the mirror and saw Keaton pressed against the surface, frowning and scanning Quinn's bedroom from the shadowy depths of Glass-Dreams. He hurried to the mirror and didn't hesitate to rest his hands against Keaton's—palm against palm, fingers neatly following their partners' positions. And it was with a tiny thrill of pleasure that Quinn realized how well their hands and fingers seemed to nearly melt into each other. Keaton's look of surprise and worry immediately eased into a big, beautiful smile of joy that lit up his face and made Quinn's insides liquefy hopelessly.

Never mind the fact that the cold spot in front of the mirror was excruciating to feel, as though Bethany was throwing everything she had out there, drawing from the deepest well imaginable to make this moment possible for both her son and his savior. All hands on deck, she seemed to say. All hands on deck. And Quinn took heart from that despite the doubts that lingered.

"Hi," Quinn breathed, grinning back in astonished pleasure.

"Hi back. I thought I wouldn't be able to see you again. I kept coming back here, calling your name and waiting." Keaton swallowed, and Quinn suddenly noticed his slightly unfocused eyes bright with unshed tears.

"I've been wanting to see you again, too, but I didn't know how. I'm sorry if I took too long."

Keaton blinked rapidly, and his composure returned. Once again, Quinn wanted to swoon as silly comparisons to James Steerforth came back in full force, nearly knocking him off his feet. But such was the power of infatuation, and Quinn knew that was his current malady, if "malady" was the proper word to use for his muddled and giddy state. Not love yet—no. It was too soon, he told himself, and he found that he was fine with it.

But how long before he'd succumb to Keaton's irresistible charm, though? Beauty, gentleman-like manners, and openness were all well and good, but Keaton also had struck hard with the easy revelation of his naïveté and especially the vulnerability bubbling so close to such a nearly perfect surface. And Quinn found himself horribly outgunned in that, his own loneliness rendering him too defenseless against the stirrings in his heart.

It was fast turning into a hard struggle within himself, and he dared not give in to something more than infatuation because he knew he needed to keep his head and stay pragmatic. Once he managed to release Keaton from the world of lost souls, Keaton wouldn't be his. Dolores alone was home to hundreds of available and better-looking gay men, most of whom were professionals, students pursuing their degrees, young entrepreneurs, etc. Quinn couldn't even finish college and moved back to live with his grandmother, a paid mortgage the only thing allowing him to keep a full-time job at a quirky store that paid him only five dollars an hour above minimum wage.

"Quinn? What's wrong?"

Quinn blinked, the heavy, rancid fog of angst and self-loathing lifting. He found himself sagging against the mirror, his head turned so that the side of his face rested on the glass where Keaton's right shoulder was. Without the mirror between them, his forehead would be pressed against Keaton's neck.

"Wha—oh. Oh, shit. Sorry. I kind of..."

*Now, kiddo. Now.*

The whisper sounded so close, yet Quinn doubted its reality all the same. His brain was sagging under the weight of so many thoughts—past, present, future, possibilities, impossibilities, self-pity, self-directed annoyance at all that self-pity—that nothing currently touching his senses felt real. He had to pull himself together, he chided himself. He couldn't afford to dilly-dally and play the tragic figure in a surreal adventure.

Pushing himself away from the mirror felt—strange. His hands, palms still flat against the glass, seemed to lose their grip somehow because the more he pushed, the more insubstantial the mirror felt. Like cold, melting butter, the glass slowly and steadily gave way under his weight, and Quinn sank—for that was the only word he could think of—forward.

"Quinn?"

"Keaton?"

*It'll be all right. Relax, sweetheart. Relax. You can do this.*

Quinn tried to scramble to right himself, but gravity and magic won out in the end, and he sank into the mirror with a horrified cry. Everything unfolded in a torturously slow and almost lazy way, with Quinn's panic spiraling wildly even as it felt as though he'd gotten detached from himself and was now objectively watching the catastrophe happen through the filter of a movie camera. One that, of course, played everything back in slow motion.

And accidentally tumbling into the world of Glass-Dreams felt like flailing through a thick but easily yielding wall of icy jelly, the transition from the mortal world to that of the dead making Quinn's ears pop. He also wasn't sure, but amid his cries and the wild air distortions as the barrier was breached, he thought he heard a woman's voice weave in and out, struggling to be heard. It had shifted from urgent but reassuring whispers to a sound that was more readily understood. Now that he was, literally, in the world of the dead, a dead woman's voice had taken on qualities that were more alive and whole, when, in the world of the living, it had been nothing more than disembodied wisps of nearly incoherent words.

"Go! Go! Help!"

The awful noise fell away just as suddenly, and the chilly thickness gave way to slightly cold but normal air. Quinn's momentum almost immediately stopped. His spinning brain slowed till clarity asserted itself, and Quinn realized a warm body had just broken his fall.

"Quinn—are you all right?" Keaton stammered.

Quinn stared in mute shock at his new surroundings as he peered over Keaton's shoulder. He let out a tiny whimper of fear once he realized Keaton was holding him tightly against himself. Jerkily he freed himself from Keaton's arms and had to take a few stumbling steps back in order to gape at the young man in Victorian dress who now also gaped back at him.

"What—what—oh, my God," Quinn whispered, and he pressed a hand against his mouth. It was a miracle he hadn't hyperventilated yet and possibly fainted as a result.

"Quinn," Keaton whispered back. "How did you do that?"

Quinn instinctively spun around to look at the mirror, and his heart nearly stopped.

A woman stood on the other side where he'd just been. She appeared to be young—no older than her early twenties—and her gaunt face was marred with bruises, her hair unkempt as though it had been blown by a strong wind, and her head's alignment with her shoulders appeared wrong. And yet, for all the gruesome features presented to a terrified Quinn, he couldn't help but feel a wave of pity and grief at the sight of Keaton's mother as she pinned him with a gaze filled with sadness and longing.

Her mouth moved spasmodically as she tried to speak, but no voice came out. All the same, Quinn could feel her plea like a knife cut in his chest. The voiceless dead reaching out to him as he stood in the world of the aimless dead, which now served as a solid and unyielding conduit to her—to Bethany.

"Your voice. It was clear just a second ago. What happened?" Quinn stammered.

Bethany only managed a faint smile, and Quinn understood it was sheer exhaustion that now consumed her ghost. She seemed to be barely hanging on now, but she braved it, anyway, because she wasn't quite done conveying her message to him.

*Go. Help.*

"How? I'm—stuck here! How the hell did I get in? And how do I get out?"

Bethany tapped the glass with a thin finger, and the pleading look in her ghostly eyes turned into one of desperate intensity.

*Wait. Wait for seven.*

"Seven? Seven—what, hours? Minutes?"

Panic surged when he saw Bethany's form fading.

"Bethany, wait! Seven what?"

She also appeared to be aware of her waning presence, even shaking her head in an awkward way as she chuckled softly. A very human display of resignation to the inevitable, Quinn thought. Her gaze immediately moved away from Quinn and fixed itself on Keaton, who stood just behind him. Her terrifying, haunting visage then changed, softening into tenderness, a heartbreakingly potent love directed at the orphaned young man who apparently knew nothing about her. Not to mention the horrors she'd endured to protect him from a father who could have easily hurt him beyond help.

Quinn watched as an echo of the doting mother she'd once been gave her dead features a faint semblance of life. Even her mouth, cracked and ringed with bruises, softened into another little smile.

*So handsome. My boy. My baby. All grown up now.*

"Bethany..."

She didn't bother looking back at Quinn, her gaze firmly on her silent and baffled son.

*You'll take good care of him, won't you?*

A complete sentence—a question—thrown out there in a last-ditch effort at communication. Bethany must have taken what was left of her energy and strength to ask that, and Quinn's throat tightened as he nodded. Never mind the fact that Bethany wasn't even looking at him anymore. He simply couldn't find his voice quickly enough and hoped his silence wouldn't be mistaken for hesitation or a negative.

Her thin body shook as she sighed, and Quinn thought he heard a faint sob as she finally vanished. For the next several seconds, Quinn stood in stunned silence, his wide-eyed gaze unblinking as he stared at his empty attic room at the other side of the mirror.

His throat loosened, at last, and he nodded again. "I will," he murmured. "We all will. I promise."

# Chapter 15

"I swear, I didn't see anyone," Keaton said, and that being the third time he made that claim, Quinn was forced to ease up on the desperate haranguing and let things go.

"Okay. That's okay."

Actually, it wasn't okay because it left Quinn lost and adrift with nothing for him to work with if saving Keaton was his main purpose for being forced into Glass-Dreams. He didn't even know what in blazes "seven" meant besides time. Bethany never acknowledged even that bit of rather important information, but, again, Quinn couldn't help but be convinced it had everything to do with time.

His mind chasing after one idea after another, he only vaguely took note of his new surroundings at the moment, though the old bewildering scent of aging paper and wood never escaped his notice. Time, he told himself. Time, time, time, time, and, yes, *time*. Wait for seven—hours? It had to be hours. Something told him seven minutes were a laughable measure in his new adventures. It simply wasn't enough time for him—in tandem with help from Bethany, that is—to gather enough...

Enough what, exactly? Energy? Power? Magic of some sort?

Seven, yes—the magic number. Seven hours required for Bethany, very likely, to regenerate and renew. Quinn and Keaton would need all the regenerated supernatural energy they could get if they wanted to get out of Glass-Dreams in one piece. Quinn needed to calm down. He needed to find his center again and keep his head, clear it of unnecessary, dramatic clutter, and be a step or two ahead of things as much as he possibly could despite his bizarre new environment.

Quinn's head throbbed with a dull ache. He wasn't a sorcerer, didn't know the first thing about channeling magic from any source if his life depended on it. And, rather ironically, his life *did* depend on it. He knew that, somehow, he was also expected to perform some sort of magic trick from his end to help now that he was no longer in the ordinary world of ordinary mortals.

"Oh, God," he muttered, scrubbing his face with both hands as awful possibilities reared their ugly heads. "I'm going to die here. I—fuckety fuck."

A shadow descended, and warmth suddenly enveloped him. He almost instantly calmed down—until he realized it was because Keaton had moved closer and enclosed him in a gentle embrace. From shock to panic to confusion to—even more confusion, though this time with a healthy dose of embarrassment, Quinn found himself stiffening instinctively at first before relaxing in Keaton's arms and allowing himself to be held and comforted. He embraced Keaton back in an awkward circle of his arms, occasionally giving Keaton's back a clumsy pat because he'd no idea what to do while being hugged by a flesh-and-blood literary wet dream who might or might not be under some form of a dark spell.

And as he held Keaton, he found just how thin the young man was, and it was a great deal more alarming than he'd first thought. Keaton was, quite likely, barely holding on to life despite the strange power that kept him functional, knowledgeable, and articulate. Quinn's throat tightened again in a surge of emotion that was now proving to be more and more difficult to tamp down.

"Five o'clock," he stammered against Keaton's shoulder.

"Hmm?"

"The time—I remember looking at the clock after I left a note for Grandma, and it said five."

Keaton hesitated. "Um—all right."

"If your mom said wait for seven, she meant wait for seven hours, which would make it midnight."

Midnight. The witching hour. But of course, Quinn thought with a heavy mental sigh. Why on earth not? It was the only logical conclusion, especially with the magical number seven in play.

Keaton took another brief moment before speaking again. "For what?"

"To get you out of here."

Keaton released him then, but he kept his hands on Quinn's shoulders, fixing him in place as he looked steadily into Quinn's eyes. "Why would I want to leave now that you're here with me? I'm not alone anymore. I finally have someone to grow old with."

He then moved his hands and explored Quinn's face with tentative and gentle touches, a hint of wonder and joy woven into every graze, every skim of Keaton's fingers over Quinn's cheeks, eyelids, nose, and mouth. It was almost blasphemous, the way Keaton's touches seemed to worship Quinn's features.

Even the way he carefully pulled Quinn's glasses off spoke of awe and even adoration.

At the same time, though, Keaton's words hung heavily in the air, and Quinn's initial horror took a little too long to turn into denial. Even as he allowed Keaton to touch him reverently, his entire being surged in huffy rebellion.

"Uh—no," he said once he found his voice. He immediately plucked his glasses from Keaton's loose hold and put them back on. "That's not how it works in *my* world, buddy. You don't belong here, and your mom wants you back in one healthy piece." He pinched his mouth and then muttered, "And she dumped this job on me. It's like if we don't get our asses out of here when midnight hits, we turn into a pair of dumb pumpkins."

"Oh. But what would I have out there? I'm a foundling. I don't have a family to come home to. Over here, I'm doing pretty well. I'm just—lonely, I guess."

"Your mom's kind of out there, waiting."

"But I didn't see her."

"Um—yeah. That's—that's because she's also kind of dead. It's her ghost that helped bring me here."

"Oh," Keaton replied, and that was that, strangely enough.

Quinn had enough time to observe his companion closely now that he was in Keaton's world, and what he saw made him more uneasy than before. Keaton might talk intelligently or seem lucid, but his features, up close, betrayed a worrisome state of dreaminess—a lot more vivid and intense than when viewed through the hazy filter of an enchanted mirror. His eyes had about them a faraway look, a faint glassiness that made Quinn think of someone who'd been hexed up, down, and sideways, which, in a way, pretty much summed up poor Keaton's entire life up to that moment.

And perhaps that was the nature of life in a world of lost souls. A mortal who shouldn't live in such a world for as long as Keaton did had predictably absorbed some of the magic that fully defined Glass-Dreams. In a way, it made Keaton something like a hybrid, a young man who was mortal yet had taken on some immortal qualities. Quinn went further and mulled over Efrain Thorley's theories about the nature of Glass-Dreams and its doomed inhabitants—theories that, apparently, were easily provable from Quinn's end now. And so just like his knowledge of the mortal world, Keaton had absorbed remnants of past lives—education, manners, even values, to a point—from the hundred or even thousands of souls still lingering in a dark and static world.

Just like Glass-Dreams, Keaton grew up to be what he now was through a passive process, a gradual absorption or osmosis of residual traces of humanity. Like a mortal sponge soaking up immortal essences. And because of that, Keaton's physical presence had also been affected, and he appeared as though his mind was elsewhere, lost in a pretty, languid dream, even while he interacted relatively normally with Quinn.

And that could also be the reason why Keaton looked and behaved the way he did: a puzzling yet entrancing mix of modern and outdated.

That led Quinn to the awful conclusion that the very same thing could happen to him if he ended up stuck in Glass-Dreams. There was no way he was going to let it, and though he'd nothing solid to go by but outlandish theories, he knew he simply needed to trust Bethany. Intuition demanded it, and he knew better than to ignore it. In a world like Glass-Dreams, the rules were different, and logic either had no place here or was turned on its head, completely redefined to mirror the nature of a dark world.

"Okay," Quinn said at length, frowning as determination reasserted itself. He stepped away from Keaton and strode to the mirror, taking in his reflection. The magic had died down, apparently, and the mirror was now back to its original state. "If I'm going to be stuck here for seven hours, I guess I'd better make the most of it."

He pondered for a moment and then turned around. Keaton, ever the pseudo-Victorian gentleman, stood patiently and waited, as handsome and dreamy as a trapped mortal could be handsome and dreamy, not to mention unbearably sublime and lickable in all his anachronistic glory. Quinn had to clear his throat before proceeding.

"So what do you do for fun around here?"

It was best to ignore the surrealism of the moment and simply go with the unnatural flow. Perhaps Quinn would be able to learn something important that might prove useful in his assigned task.

"Fun? Oh—there's a dance every night, though not in the same place."

Quinn blinked. "Every night? Are you serious? Damn. Don't you get sick of it?"

"You're not obligated to attend every one of them. There are many people here, so no one's going to lose out if some skip certain nights."

Keaton's memory would have to be affected by his dreams as well, and what he was now telling Quinn could easily be incorrect. Quinn suddenly remembered Keaton's vague claims about sleeping and dreaming and having one moment melt seamlessly into another—waking state and dream state together. It wouldn't be a surprise if Keaton himself ended up confused as to the nature of reality and fantasy in his ghostly world if that was the way his hours were spent.

"Uh-huh. Okay." Quinn paused and gazed around him, his hands on his hips. "What kind of dances? No, wait. I think I know. Do you waltz in grand ballrooms and stuff?"

Keaton's faint, indulgent smile widened, and his eyes almost sparkled. Almost. Maybe it was nothing more than dead people magic imbuing him with a soft, ethereal glow, Quinn thought dubiously. He hoped he wasn't going to regret pursuing this idea, let alone encouraging Keaton, which apparently pleased the latter.

All the same, he couldn't keep himself from gawping at Keaton like a moonstruck teenager.

"Suck me dry, you're hot when you smile at me like that," he whispered.

"Would you like me to teach you how to waltz?"

Seven hours, Quinn reminded himself when another wave of doubt swept over him. He had seven hours to spend there, and unless Keaton knew how to play strip poker and keep him happily occupied for that insane length of time, holing himself in the attic room and watching the mirror for seven hours would definitely be a terrible, terrible thing.

On the one hand, the thought of venturing out into a world of aimless souls, a world whose very essence was that of death, echoes of human lives, and eerie, organic kind of magic born of its residents, made Quinn's stomach twist itself into a painfully tight corkscrew. There were too many unknown variables out there ready to make his unplanned visit to Glass-Dreams a living—and possibly a permanent—hell.

On the other hand, Quinn had to admit to being nervous but curious about the world of lost souls. He could definitely learn something about it, share it with Efrain and help him in his calling. Other than Keaton, who was there solely by accident and wasn't even fully aware of the significance (not to mention logistics) of his presence in that world, Quinn was an active participant in this—momentary visit. He was clearly aware of his new environment and could interact with it as he saw fit, especially in the capacity of temporary protector to Keaton.

And the reckless part of him sniffed and pawed away at his consciousness, pleading to be let out for a quick jaunt and piddle in the backyard. *Go on, run with it,* a voice seemed to whisper excitedly into his ear, and Quinn took a deep breath and dove right in.

"Okay," he said with a tight grin. "Why not? Knowing how to waltz might end up being a pretty useful skill out there. Back in the real world, I mean."

"Great. Now—oh, sorry. Forgot my manners."

With a sweet blush, Keaton walked up to Quinn and offered his arm. It took a couple of seconds for Quinn's brain to get with the program, and flashes of images from period dramas he'd seen kicked his mind into gear. Of course, only a well-bred gentleman would offer his arm gallantly to his partner.

Quinn thought about Matt and the others, and he muttered, "Suck on this, bitches."

"May I?" Keaton asked, and Quinn took the proffered arm, practically blushing and tittering, feeling more and more like a giddy tween being whisked away by his secret crush. Since he wasn't feeling as though he were close to swooning into Keaton's arms, maybe his self-control around hot young men was improving.

# Chapter 16

"What—what happened?"

"You swooned."

The world seemed to throb in a way that called to mind arrhythmia to Quinn. Keaton sat on the uneven and uncomfortable ground, his lap serving as a pillow. Shockingly, he was also stroking Quinn's hair with a calming, rhythmic gentleness that eased the dizzy cloudiness warping Quinn's brain. With a slightly trembling hand, Quinn adjusted his glasses and stared at the sky, which turned out to be a rather undesirable thing to do. The clouds, a collection of shredded pale gray cotton moving in lethargic swirls against a vividly violet sky, made him dizzy all over again, and he was forced to close his eyes against the view while struggling to sit up.

"I don't swoon," he stammered.

"You did. Over here we call it 'the vapors' or something. I admit it's pretty fetching when you do it."

Quinn took his glasses off and rubbed his eyes. He caught himself before he could blurt out "only girls faint" and get into a bit of trouble with Keaton and/or his conscience. But everything felt so wrong, from the dizziness and disorientation to the immeasurably deep sensation of the world being hopelessly askew. That one went beyond Quinn's gut. It seemed to have been fully absorbed by every atom of his body, the actual physicality of such wrongness giving it a terrifying edge. And Quinn would have been reduced to a trembling mass of incoherent gibberish if it weren't for the fact he also wanted to throw up everything he'd consumed since he was a mere glint in his father's eye.

"There's nothing fetching about wanting to puke before passing out," Quinn said as Keaton, now on his feet, gently helped him stand up. "Why the hell am I so dizzy? I mean—I felt kind of off when we were in your room, but it's like the farther we are from your home, the more messed up I feel."

Keaton looked suitably baffled. "I don't know. Maybe it's because you're not used to this place. Stands to reason, right?"

"I guess."

Quinn's response was reluctant at best. His dizziness and fogginess were physical responses to an abnormal world, yes, but there was something about

Glass-Dreams that didn't sit well with him—besides the fact it was a world of ghosts, that is. Perhaps it was nothing more than a product of his more-addled-than-usual brain, but Quinn thought he sensed a quiet malignance in the air, one that, somehow, he knew permeated every black rock and the barely visible ground mist. And now that he was attuned to this vague, teasing kind of malevolence, the less he felt the need to venture out and learn what he could of Keaton's adopted world.

Perhaps the world of the lost dead wasn't meant to be parsed, dissected, stuck under a sorcerer's microscope, and studied within an inch of its not-quite life. Quinn, for his part, felt more and more convinced such was the case, and he wasn't one to argue against common sense.

"Where are we, anyway?"

"On our way to tonight's ball. We're not too far off. Just follow everyone. See? It's not like we're on our own here."

Quinn at first didn't understand what Keaton had just said and gazed around him. The countryside—if one were to call it that—outside Keaton's home called to mind wild, brooding moors with its rugged and relentlessly undulating ground, gorse brush liberally peppering the area, and the restless winds that kept blowing.

And with the winds came the heavy, overpowering smell of earth, wood, and leaf. A familiar smell, of course, as it was the same one he'd experienced in the ruined house next door to his home. The only difference between the two places was the fact that within the ruins, the air was stagnant and thick, almost suffocating in its strange solidity. As if the presence of the mortal world had forced it back into its corner and encased it in an invisible but solid container, keeping things rigidly secure and making Quinn call to mind images of snow globes. In Glass-Dreams, the smell seemed even more alive and active and yet just as trapped. The feeling of a sentient environment Quinn had felt among the ruins was also present, but the landscape imbued it with a more alarming mix of confusion and a perpetual edginess. He thought of an aging wild animal pacing endlessly within its massive pen.

There were a number of dead, twisted trees also littering the landscape, the thin ground mist providing just the right kind of punctuation at the end of a very gothic scene. Quinn, who'd seen every adaptation of *Jane Eyre* imaginable, knew a bleak moor when he saw one, though he did find the presence of trees a strange anomaly. As far as he knew, moors were quite open and wild, with no trees anywhere. Then again, anything was possible in Glass-Dreams.

He thought about his grandmother's patterns, recalling those details involving funerary statuary and other things. None of those, to his amazement, were present in any way, and not even a determined squinting to catch whatever stood or lay in the distance yielded anything. Everything was just as barren and bleak as ever, and he now wondered if what his grandmother had sewn was nothing more than a representation of the world of the lost dead, not a literal picture of it.

In fact, that detail about the two figures staring at each other through a single window could only be him and Keaton, the window representing the mirror. The smaller female figure would have to be Bethany, hovering just behind Quinn, ever watchful and patient. As for the other figure, well, he'd yet to figure that one out, and he had to admit to himself that he wasn't too keen on discovering the truth of that horrible, misshapen thing.

Quinn blew out a breath to force his mind back to the moment, and he gave the scenery another thorough look. And as far as he could see, it was only Keaton and him present there.

"I don't get it," he said after a moment. "What're you talking about? Everyone? Unless you're tripping, I don't see anyone else out here." He waved a hand vaguely.

"Really?" Keaton gazed around him. "You don't see them? Oh, hello, Francis. Haven't seen you in a while. Looks like you had your hair professionally done. You look wonderful, too, Gwendolyn. Oh—you're welcome. It's my pleasure as always, and you know how flattering that dress has always been to your figure."

Quinn's mouth hung slack as he watched Keaton casually interact with invisible people.

"Oh, hell," he murmured, feeling the blood drain away from him. He cleared his throat just as Keaton grinned at something and waved at it almost shyly. "Um—Keaton? Who're you talking to?"

"My friends," Keaton replied matter-of-factly and without a second's hesitation. He held his hands behind him as he nodded now and then, acknowledging unseen people as they apparently ambled past. "They're all on their way to the ball. Actually, they're late, but it doesn't really matter. People come and go, and everyone has fun. Hello, Will—did you put on weight or something?"

Quinn tried to be a really good sport about it and tamped down the overriding urge to panic. Taking a deep, calming breath, he casually moved into what he believed to be the path taken by Keaton's not-quite-imaginary friends. It was, in fact, a dirt path he could barely see in the cover of the night, though the moon's cold and faint beams helped chase some of the shadows away. He didn't know where the path began—not that it mattered, at any rate, considering where they were—but Quinn did notice it snaked over the undulating terrain with no side paths to be seen anywhere, and it even went past Keaton's home from what he remembered.

As the wind continued to blow, he stretched out an arm and did his best to focus.

The winds were tolerably cool on the whole, but there was also a faint iciness that wove itself as extremely fine and random currents. For a brief moment Quinn dismissed them as nothing more than a natural part of the restless movements of the night air.

But the more he opened himself to his environment, the more he realized how mistaken he was. Those random icy currents had a certain quality of wrongness to them, an unnatural essence that was both an ordinary part of Glass-Dreams and yet was also a distinctive abnormality, for lack of a better term. And after another moment spent opening himself up to the world of the aimless dead, he realized the malignance he'd sensed earlier was there, and it *was* the wrongness he now felt in the chilly currents.

"Oh! Ouch!"

He hissed and snatched his hand away, holding it protectively against his chest as he stared in dumbfounded silence at the emptiness next to him.

"Quinn? What happened? Are you all right?"

"Uh—nothing. Just the wind, I guess. It got too cold for a few seconds to the point where it actually hurt. Like a freezing kind of burn."

Quinn grimaced as he nursed his hand, and he glanced at Keaton to find him observing his unseen friends with an air of confusion. Keaton didn't speak, though Quinn could sense a purposeful suppression roiling inside him, as if the young man was weighed down with more and more questions but fought back the need to give voice to them. Keaton frowned as he watched his friends move past them, his eyes tracking their progress. Then he turned his attention back to Quinn, his body language a little stiff and tense, his manner wary and unsure.

"Are you ready to dance?" Keaton asked when Quinn made his way back to his side. Even his smile appeared stiff and riddled with doubt as he offered Quinn his arm again.

"What's going on, Keaton?"

Quinn dropped his voice when he spoke, now fully attuned to his companion's odd behavior. The unease he felt from a moment or so ago remained, and it seemed to have ramped up in strength. Now and then, a chilly sting would make him falter in his pace as he walked side-by-side with Keaton. And with that chilly sting came that awful undercurrent of malevolence, one that he wondered was aimed at him.

"I'm not really sure," Keaton replied in a matching whisper. He kept sneaking glances around them, the shadow of confusion deepening further. "Some of them are—uh—acting strange."

Quinn winced at another icy sting that felt like a quick knife cut into his cheek. When he touched his face experimentally, his fingers came away unmarked with blood. That, at least, was a relief.

"What do you mean strange?"

"Agitated. Restless. And—not all of them are like that, though." Keaton paused to observe a little more, moving his free hand to rest it on Quinn's as Quinn held his arm like before. His hand was warm, its weight a comforting and protective one. "Maybe it's nothing. Everyone else seems to be fine, though."

A rather tense silence fell, with Quinn's hair rising on end at the unbearable eeriness of the moment. Nothing had changed at least in his immediate surroundings. And yet a creeping dread was now making itself felt, raising his heart rate, causing goosebumps to break out all over again, forcing him to engage all senses.

Ah, yes, there it was—one disturbing development in a string of disturbing developments.

Voices.

Distant, sporadically audible, and even then, pale and feeble enough to rouse even more doubts in Quinn's mind. He couldn't discern words—only sounds, both male and female. He couldn't tell if they were cries or shouts, or there was some strong emotion woven into those brief and random tones. The overall effect was even more unnerving since it almost seemed like hearing distant, disembodied conversations echoing up and down a deserted landscape and he couldn't determine the direction of the voices' source.

"So—can you describe their movements?" he whispered, determined to keep going despite the overwhelming urge to turn around and march right back to Keaton's home and the safety of his attic room.

"Breaking ranks. They all normally follow a single path to the ball, but—some are wandering off, looking confused and lost. Some are—well, they're agitated. Irritable. I can see their faces, and the agitated ones are—well, they're looking straight at you."

Keaton's voice faltered.

"They can see me?"

"No one could before when you started your walk to the dance, but—hey, stop that! Back off!"

Quinn yelped when something touched his arm, and the feeling of invisible fingers wrapping around it were so cold that they burned. They ended just as quickly as they started, however, but the impression they left was strong enough for Quinn to nearly beg Keaton to hurry along. Keaton didn't need to think twice, and he kept his hand pressed against Quinn's as he increased their pace. Now and then, he'd wave that same protective hand wildly as though shooing away unseen pests, while Quinn grimaced and endured an occasional sting and the vague malevolence he now felt that was bearing down on him from all sides.

He made a promise to Bethany, though. He told himself he wasn't about to shrink away from an invisible enemy that easily, and if push came to shove, he'd give the aimless dead a run for their money.

"Ugh," Quinn whispered upon realizing what a sad little empty threat it was. For starters, he sure wouldn't know how to defend himself and Keaton against ghosts he couldn't even see. "Famous last words, Geiger. Famous last words."

# Chapter 17

Somehow they made it to the ball despite Quinn fainting three more times and putting up with what felt like increasing attacks from invisible bullies.

"God, are we there yet?" he stammered, groaning, as Keaton helped him up to his feet after his final recovery. "I don't think I can take any more of this just to learn how to waltz."

His arms felt raw, in a way, his skin aching where unseen hands had tried to grip him as though in angry warning. Keaton, bless his gallant soul, had also managed to fend off those not-quite-attacks with angry reproofs and even an occasional hand-swat aimed at something only he could see. Quinn's face, or at least his cheeks, also felt a touch raw from where icy-hot fingers had tried to touch him. Keaton had inspected his face now and then, a shadow of worry darkening his features whenever he described faint red marks left on Quinn's skin.

He'd offered to turn around and take Quinn back several times throughout their eventful trek to the ball, but Quinn had resisted, for better or for worse, convinced he needed to venture as far out as he could from Keaton's home and explore the land of Glass-Dreams. He could learn something valuable; that single thought had urged him forward with his stupendously insane scheme to carry on as though nothing borderline dangerous was hounding his every step. If he was ordered to hang around a horrifying abnormality of a world as Glass-Dreams, there was surely a purpose for it.

And something deep in his gut told him he was going in the right direction: always forward, not back, no matter what might lie ahead. For whatever reason, instinct firmly seated its baffling posterior on the notion that whatever Quinn was doing, no matter how deceptively trivial, was really important for Keaton's sake.

"Well, duh..."

"What? Did you say something?"

"Nah. Just clearing my throat. So, uh, where's the—okay, you're joshing me, right?"

Keaton blinked. "No. This is it. Why, were you expecting something else?"

"Um—yeah?"

Quinn had expected standard ballroom stuff from historical dramas, with grand palatial settings, glittering lights, and men and women all dressed to the nines, swirling around and around to the tune of pretty tunes in three-fourths time. He'd expected laughter, beauty, and near-perfection, with costumes that made his eyeballs dangle helplessly from their sockets.

Instead he found himself gaping at a fantastically designed folly standing in stark relief against an unearthly countryside. In the middle of a rugged and bleak moor, the small building appeared like a badly misplaced relic from history, its architectural details calling to mind glorious medieval churches. Quinn remembered something along those lines in one of his classes—some English politician and writer with a fetish for the gothic and who was born with enough money to satisfy his whims, so that he'd had a faux-medieval villa built for his pleasure. The folly boasted classic gothic features like pointed arches and rose windows, looking like a miniature cathedral—but also on its way to collapsing on one's head, judging from the cracks, sagging portions of the roof, and the ubiquitous vines that seemed to be the only things holding the entire structure together.

There, too, was ghostly yellow-orange light feebly pouring out of the windows.

"Are you sure?" he blurted out once he found his voice. "That's the place?"

"Yeah. What's the matter?"

Quinn had half a mind to demand how hundreds or thousands of ghosts could possibly fit themselves in a small folly like that, but he managed to derail himself with the rather important word *ghosts*. With a tired sigh, he rolled his eyes at himself.

A crowd the size of Napoleon's army could easily fit inside a small structure like this. Ghosts never jostled each other for space. They merely—overlapped, for lack of a better term, and they could dance into each other all night long without erupting into intangible fist fights over rude manhandling, an occasional elbow digging into someone's side or kidneys, and toes getting stepped on.

"Nothing, nothing. Uh—are your friends going to be okay with me crashing the party? They weren't exactly thrilled meeting me on the way here."

Keaton hesitated before the door of the folly, and he looked around them, gently removing his arm from Quinn's hold and sliding it down and around his waist instead. Quinn noticed Keaton didn't bother with a side hug and an arm around his shoulders. For that he was grateful as his own arms continued to smart from what felt like endless ghostly touches. With a grimace, he wondered how his limbs looked after coming into contact with irritable spirits despite the—admittedly flimsy—protection of his cotton hoodie. He expected to see red imprints in the shape of hands, and with any luck, a quick and frantic phone call to Efrain Thorley would lead him to get some proper magical healing. Though, of course, he also expected Efrain to poke and prod, in a way, and shove him under a sorcerer's microscope for intensive study before healing him.

"I'll take care of you," Keaton replied in a low and quiet voice.

"I know you will. You have been since I crossed over and passed out a gazillion times."

Quinn turned his face to look at Keaton, the ongoing dizziness and confusion momentarily giving way to wonder and admiration. Keaton was very much like a gentleman, whatever behavior and ideas he'd absorbed throughout his years in Glass-Dreams working quite magically for him. And it was a thing of beauty and a great puzzle to boot as far as Quinn was concerned—that Keaton, despite his exposure to the lost dead, had still come out a good man, a perfect balance of old and new, that he'd somehow managed to avoid absorbing negativity and misery from the souls surrounding him day in and day out.

How on earth did that work? Did Keaton's life in Glass-Dreams say something about the nature of the human soul? Or was this purely specific to those caught in the endless, aimless world of Glass-Dreams? Did this surreal limbo neutralize souls, in a manner of speaking, purging them of all faults and vices that had partly defined their natures while alive?

Were the souls in that world nothing more than remnants of hopes, dreams, and happier memories?

Or, even more fascinating to consider, was Keaton's goodness a product of some protective shielding from Bethany? Perhaps, because she was now dead, she'd managed to reach across in some way or another and be a mother to her unfortunate baby. That, somehow, she'd succeeded in nurturing him without being there or only through a fine and delicate thread connecting them in heart and spirit.

What bothered Quinn the most in all this was the too-real possibility of his never learning the truth despite his efforts. He had a feeling this was going to be one of those puzzles no one was meant to solve because there was simply no way for the dead to lay out the truth for the living to study and understand. A necromancer might, perhaps, but even Quinn, a layman, knew just how much of a huge no-no necromancy was.

The questions coming in from all sides were threatening to make Quinn swoon all over again, so he forced himself to shake off those thoughts and simply live in the moment, which included looking closely at Keaton and losing himself in the young man's dreamy gaze.

"You promise not to laugh if I mess up learning how to waltz?" he asked once he realized his awed silence was drawing itself out far too long.

"I'll never laugh at you. We all have to start somewhere, don't we? That's what I've been taught, anyway." Keaton beamed, and he caught Quinn completely off-guard by leaning close and planting a quick and chaste kiss on his mouth. "There. Is that guarantee enough?"

"Didn't expect that, but, yeah. I'll take it."

"Excellent."

"So—how'd you learn how to kiss?"

"I just know. I understand the mechanics." Keaton actually paused and appeared to carefully think over things. "Like—between two non-relations, a kiss could be friendship or love. And—you just do it."

How terribly sweet and naïve, Quinn thought, unable to help a silly little smile as he listened. Funny how the complex workings of human emotion and interaction sounded so grounded in simple common sense once stripped of all the ridiculous drama and other trappings mortals had learned to attach to them. Keaton's quiet, matter-of-fact responses worked like a much-needed breath of fresh air.

"And how did you know who to kiss?"

"Easy. I've seen some of the people here kiss each other, and it's because they're attracted. Or that's my understanding of it, anyway. I happen to be attracted to you, so—there you have it."

This learning by supernatural osmosis certainly had its quirky virtues, Quinn told himself.

Keaton, one arm still around Quinn's waist, moved toward the double doors and opened them with some trouble using his free hand, the ancient hinges groaning from the sudden, forced movement. It was all very gothic, to be sure, and Quinn pretended he was Jane Eyre with a penis and nerdy glasses that kept slipping down his nose. He nudged them back up as they entered the folly, the darkness he'd grown so used to now replaced by an odd, warm glow within, a glow whose source couldn't be seen. He looked around and saw not only an empty interior, but also one that sank visibly from the weight of old, old magic, Nature, and immortals. It was a curious, unexpected thought that crossed his mind, but there it was, and he was also convinced of it, instinct brooking no argument.

Marble floors and opulently papered walls, exquisitely detailed moulding, windows, and a painted ceiling were all cracked, faded, and overrun in places by creeping vines that had managed to find their way through fissures and holes. The folly's interior smelled of rich earth and a hint of pine, the silence feeling like a living, mournful presence.

Quinn pointedly ignored the absence of music and an orchestra, which he was sure only Keaton could see and hear. Swallowing, he turned to his would-be partner and forced a little smile. At least, he thought, he felt less disjointed and ready to lose consciousness in there. Perhaps the folly protected him from those awful influences, much like Keaton's home did. He still felt a touch woozy, but it was at least bearable and easily shrugged off.

"So—how do you waltz?" he asked, and Keaton blessed him with a big, beautiful smile.

"We hold each other like this," Keaton said, positioning one of Quinn's hands on his shoulder and the other in his right hand while he rested his left on Quinn's waist. "We don't have to follow the speed of the music yet since you're just learning, and we can hold each other a little more apart than usual until you feel comfortable enough."

Quinn nodded, feeling the heat creep up his cheeks as he once again found himself held captive by Keaton's mist-softened gaze. "Okay. I can't hear the orchestra, anyway, so I'm kind of depending on you for everything."

"You can't? Really?"

"Nope. Not a single note. This is going to be a really interesting lesson for me."

Keaton gazed around them for a second or two as though to confirm his partner's sanity or hearing ability first before moving forward. When he turned his attention back to Quinn, he offered a soft, indulgent smile.

"All right. Here we go."

And before Quinn knew it, they were slowly moving around the great room, avoiding a stumble or two somehow, and it didn't take long for him to settle comfortably into the three-fourths rhythm of the unheard music. He found, in the end, that he didn't care much. He simply enjoyed Keaton's company. He enjoyed being in Keaton's half-embrace. He enjoyed being the center of Keaton's universe if only for a brief and temporary time.

So this, he thought with equal parts breathless amazement and exhilarating joy, was what falling in love was like. He knew he was jumping the gun by thinking about love, so perhaps this was more in line with the beginnings of a deeper infatuation. He'd never been in love, but he'd had crushes in the past, and he'd always likened crushes with early blooms that never quite made it to full maturity, wilting and dying even before the petals fully opened.

This, however, was something else. If the extraordinary nature of his coming together with Keaton was a big—if not the primary—influence of his spirit-soaring epiphany, Quinn still wouldn't have anything to complain about. If anything, he believed himself lucky enough to be thrown into circumstances that would've given Edgar Allan Poe a case of ecstatic fits of artistic inspiration. Even if nothing were to come out of this between him and Keaton, he knew he was nothing if not grateful for having experienced something so unique and special despite the unnerving character of Keaton's world.

And so they waltzed and talked and laughed and waltzed some more. And the longer they danced, the more Keaton's dreaminess appeared to fade, though Quinn breathlessly suspected it was nothing more than his giddy brain playing tricks on him.

# Chapter 18

Adrenaline. Yes, that would have to be it, Quinn thought. It was adrenaline that gave him the impetus to boldly take over the dance when Keaton subtly withdrew once Quinn showed more confidence in himself. It was adrenaline that encouraged him to be playful with his partner, not just cracking jokes so he could enjoy Keaton's bright, pealing laughter, but also improvise silly steps without breaking their rhythm as they moved in a perpetual circle around the great room. Quinn never heard a single note of the ghostly waltz, but he didn't care. Keaton appeared to be open to anything Quinn threw his way, and that was really all Quinn needed.

If fairy tales were real, Quinn would liken the moment to when the enchantment was broken. In his case, it was a gradual tearing down of a lifetime of unnatural influences. Keaton's eyes, their glassy-dreaminess, had definitely cleared by slow degrees, and it was Quinn's quick thinking that got him to experiment with improvisation as a means of determining what was causing the lifting of the spell.

It appeared that unexpected turns, outlandish behavior, and anything that caught Keaton by surprise in a positive way, seemed to draw Keaton's humanity out from the mists that had kept it hidden for so long. Keaton had been swaddled in the timeless echoes of other people's experiences from lifetimes ago. Since his infancy, in fact, those shadowy remnants of lives long gone had been his world, the darker, more unfathomable magic of such a world the only force that had kept him alive all this time.

Granted, that magic was now displaying a loosening hold in Quinn's eyes, judging from Keaton's thinness, and it was quite likely the right time for some form of intervention before it was too late. Perhaps even ageless and incomprehensible magic had its own limits, an expiration date of sorts when it came to its hold on something or someone not meant to be in its world.

"And this is the tango," Quinn said, promptly changing directions and forcing his laughing partner to follow his lead. He knew nothing about dancing the tango, of course, but he'd seen enough videos only briefly, so he largely winged it. "And you're supposed to dip me like—whoa! Yeah, like that. Not too low, though. You'll hurt your back and crack my skull against the floor."

Keaton, red-faced and still laughing, drew him back to the waltz. A few more minutes of insanity on the dance floor, and both of them were fully winded, though neither showed signs of wanting to stop. Quinn didn't, anyway, and he'd like to hold Keaton close for as long as he could.

"And this is how we slow dance in the other world," he said, panting. He pulled Keaton closer, their hands keeping their positions, till they were dancing cheek to cheek. "You have to move so that it's like you're just shifting your weight from one foot to the other. Like that, yeah. You got it."

"This is weird."

"But pretty relaxing, right?" And pretty damned sweet, but Quinn wasn't about to say it out loud.

"Yes. After all that activity, it's good to ease up. I need to catch my breath."

"I'm a little too much to handle, eh?"

"That'd be an understatement."

Quinn laughed softly, eyelids fluttering shut. "You should spend some time with my grandmother and my best friend. You'll find yourself rethinking that understatement thing, and I'm sure it'll be pretty tough coming up with the appropriate word for me."

"For now: charming. Very charming. Even with your quirks." Keaton paused. "Especially because of your quirks, I should say."

Quinn merely smiled against Keaton's shoulder. He could always hum a song to guide Keaton, but it looked like his partner had taken to the new dance well enough and seemed comfortable with something quieter and more intimate. Perhaps it was the very nature of slow dancing that rendered them both mute all of a sudden, a faint nervousness flavoring the silence, but nervousness over what? Quinn couldn't answer for Keaton, but for his part, a sudden shyness overcame him, sending him down the familiar path of self-consciousness and crippling doubt.

He wished he didn't feel so inadequate, but he couldn't help it. It was one thing to admire someone from afar, weaving romantic fantasies in his head, where everything was safe and well within his control. Should the object of his admiration find someone whom he wished to court, Quinn's heart was safe. Well, safe-*r*, anyway, because even if he were to feel some pain, it wouldn't be anywhere near the crippling levels of actual heartbreak that could only come from actual contact with the other person. Yes, it was one thing to admire from afar; it was entirely another to be placed in the line of fire like this.

*Ah, forget it. Let it go, man. Let it go. It's not about you. This is all for him.*

He turned his attention to his surroundings instead, allowing Keaton to take over and feel even more comfortable holding someone close. With any luck, Keaton would be able to assimilate in the mortal world more easily than he'd first hoped, and perhaps this ongoing contact with Quinn would be a step in the right direction, however tiny that step might be. There was so much of the mortal world Keaton had to be brought up to speed with, and with a pang, Quinn wondered whether or not Keaton's naïveté and goodness would be able to stand up to the varied expressions of human nature awaiting him out there. Hopefully someone with some understanding of Keaton's unusual situation would take him under their wing and help him through the adjustment and re-education. Quinn might not want to be hurt, but it was another matter entirely, thinking of Keaton being hurt by living, breathing people.

"What's wrong?" Keaton asked, his quiet voice a gentle nudge back to the present.

"Huh? Oh—nothing. Just losing myself in this. How about you?"

"Same here. I thought I heard you mumble something, though."

"Nah. I just make weird sounds when I think no one's paying me any attention."

They stopped, and for the briefest moment, they simply stood there, in the middle of the ghostly ruins of a folly, surrounded by magic and death and infinity. No music, no other sounds other than their quiet breathing broke the silence.

Quinn wasn't at first sure what Keaton wanted to do, and he was about to pull away to ask when Keaton himself moved ever so slightly apart if only to rest his forehead against Quinn's and smile down at him.

"I like this," he said. "I really enjoy your company. I don't think I've laughed this much for—well, ever. Pretty sad, huh?"

Quinn, his face burning, managed a teeny little smile in return. "It's fun, isn't it? I'm sorry your friends never—"

Keaton kissed him then, a firm and confident press of lips that almost immediately turned into something more passionate. Mouths opened against each other, tongues snaked out and tasted, soft sighs mingled with increasingly irregular breaths. Keaton's hands released Quinn's and moved unerringly around his waist, pulling him close, and Quinn—after the initial stunned hesitation at being really, officially kissed for the first time—that is, kissed as a means of actually communicating something real and not just an experiment between two teenagers—clung to Keaton with his hands gliding up the other's back till they rested against his shoulders, fingers splayed.

They were moving fast. Way too fast, Quinn's frazzled brain noted in a blasé and dismissive tone, and it immediately sank back under the warm, delightful waves of a young man's first romantic experience.

Romantic? Yes, romantic.

*You only live once,* his mind appended with a pleased and self-indulgent purr. *Run with it.*

The air moved around them, and the temperatures dropped sharply. Quinn's eyes flew open, and his gasp of pain was muffled by Keaton's lips. One stab of icy pain followed another, and Quinn fought himself loose from Keaton's hold, stumbling away and flailing as he fended off invisible attackers.

"Ow! Keaton! Help me!"

"Stop! What're you people doing to him? I said stop it!"

There seemed to be a wild rush of chilly air mixing it up with their shouts and cries, but Quinn thought he caught other voices in the turbulence. More distinct voices this time compared to those he thought he'd heard outside, that is. There was a distinct edge of rage in them, a fury that terrified him.

They'd noticed him again—unlike those spirits on the road to the folly, these ones seemed not to sense him at all till now. Invisible hands whose touch burned horribly came at him from every direction, clawing away at his face, his arms, and his body. Many managed to take a hold of his arms, their awful grip painful and tight for a few seconds before they faded away as though the ghosts had used up whatever energy they'd been harnessing in order to attack him physically.

"Keaton! It hurts!"

Keaton swore—there was first time for everything, apparently—and pulled Quinn away, this time wrapping an arm around his shoulders and running toward the doors.

"Let's go," he barked. "No! Stop! Stay away from him!"

They just about broke the double doors down in their haste, but at least the exit wasn't barred. They ran down the road again, the night looking no different from before. Quinn's eyes blurred from tears of pain, and he gritted his teeth as he tried to ignore the ongoing assault on him, though at least this time outside the folly, the horrific touches were fewer and farther between. The dizziness and disorientation bore down on him yet again, however, and it took Quinn everything he had to keep himself upright and moving despite the threat of stumbling and collapsing in a faint.

"Why're they doing this?" he yelled, his words broken from his gasps and terrified whimpers. "I didn't do anything!"

"They saw you, Quinn," Keaton replied, panting as he refused to let up on their pace. "I don't understand. They ignored you for a good long time at first, but the longer you stayed, the more they grew aware of you, it looked like."

"But why attack me?"

"I don't know. I'm sorry. I wish I knew."

"I wasn't doing anything to hurt them."

"No, you weren't. You did nothing wrong."

Maybe he did and yet he didn't, Quinn thought, gasping and yelping in pain now and then. He'd done something wrong in the eyes of the lost dead by actively interacting with Keaton, breaking his partner's monotonous existence with unexpected and improvised dances.

There was also shared laughter and a good deal of that, too. Everything Quinn had done in Glass-Dreams ran counter to its static nature, had disrupted a rhythm that was infinite, immeasurable, and fixed. Everything he'd done was nothing more than ordinary things a mortal would do under certain circumstances, so that would be where he'd say he'd done nothing wrong.

To complicate matters further, it seemed as though Quinn had angered the ghosts of Glass-Dreams by simply existing.

Was it because he was a living, breathing mortal who'd just trespassed the world of the lost dead? Keaton had been adopted, had grown up among ghosts, who'd perhaps saw him as no different from themselves. They *were* rudderless phantasms, after all. If any awareness or understanding they had remained in death and especially in such a limbo, it would be faint or scattered, barely kept together by shadows or echoes of their former selves.

Keaton had always been one of them, in a way, however tenuous their absorption of his presence might be, and Quinn could only deduce that a *second* warm-blooded, real live person encroaching in a world not meant for him had simply created a greater imbalance. He'd disturbed the dynamics of a world that had already gone slightly askew with the presence of Keaton. He'd tipped the boat even more, so to speak, and now all hands were on the proverbial haunted deck, working hard to rid their world of an unwanted interloper.

That was a wild, frantic guess on Quinn's part, but it made too much terrifying sense.

And things almost instantly blew up in his face when they kissed, just as Keaton was slowly, slowly emerging from the darkly magical fugue state he'd always been in. The spell had been broken, and the dead were *not* amused.

# Chapter 19

"God—are we there yet? Again?" Quinn groaned, and while he'd normally force himself up and push forward for the safety of Keaton's home, he was now so, so tired and sore. All he wished for this time was to turn on his side, go fetal, and snooze his troubles away.

"Actually, we are."

"What? Really? How'd I—oh, my fuckety hell, you carried me, didn't you? I was out cold in your arms and stuff?"

"Like a momentarily comatose damsel in distress."

"Not funny." Quinn frowned in hazy confusion. "I wasn't too heavy for you?"

"No. I guess I was too anxious to get you indoors to worry about your weight. By the way, you're pretty light."

"Not *that* light. I'm sure that's your adrenaline levels talking."

Keaton snickered softly. "I don't care. I just wanted to get you inside and safe."

Quinn blinked away the haze and saw that they were, indeed, back in Keaton's home. More specifically, the bottom step of the first flight of stairs, where Keaton—bless his excessively gallant heart—had decided to stop and rest. He'd perched himself on the bottom step and kept Quinn close, cradled in his arms and draped across his lap. Like a surrealist homosexual take on the Pieta theme, Quinn had to add.

When he looked up at Keaton, he flushed at the unguarded expression of shocked pleasure that seemed to make Keaton's features glow. There was clarity and alertness in those keen eyes—no cloud of distraction or fog of distant dreams. Even the sickly pale hue of his bony face had disappeared, leaving in its wake a faint hint of rosiness, though the hopeful sign of better health made the contrasting shadows under his eyes and the slightly sunken cheeks appear even more vivid.

That said, Keaton simply looked—human. Alive. Normal. Quinn couldn't help a tired smile as he raised a hand and gently touched Keaton's face, fingers tracing a light and inarticulate trail everywhere. He wondered how Keaton would look in the full bloom of health, and while he was still a little foggy headed, he pictured Keaton looking absolutely stunning. But trouble was still nipping at their heels judging from the sounds coming from the front door.

"I think we should barricade ourselves in your attic," he said as he finally sat up, though not without a baleful look directed at the door. "Sounds like a posse's out there with torches and pitchforks and the whole shit."

"You know, I don't think I've ever seen anyone carry around torches, lamps, or candles. We never really needed extra light here."

Quinn rubbed his temples and felt the tenseness ease up a little. "Lucky you. Over at the other side, we're getting slapped left and right with electric bills. Then again, we're kind of upright and breathing over there, too, so there's that."

"Okay, there you go. Easy now." Keaton appeared not to pay Quinn's semilogical rambling any heed. He gently took Quinn's hand and held on tightly. "Come along now."

They both stumbled to their feet and hurried up the stairs, which groaned and sagged under their combined weight and their rapid and heavy steps.

The noise coming from outside was mostly weak scraping and thuds, as though phantom hands desperately worked to gain entry by gripping—and failing at gripping—the doorknob. And for the briefest moment, Quinn found himself feeling a touch sorry for ghosts. In some absurd way, they made him think of insubstantial zombies pawing ineffectively away at the locked door.

"Do your friends ever get in your house?" he asked. They'd reached the second floor and were making their way to the last flight of stairs leading to the attic room.

"Sure. I don't have to let them in, largely. They usually find a way inside one way or another, and I'm used to it. It never bothered me," Keaton replied, sounding a little out of breath by now. "Hang on. Let me catch my breath."

"You let them storm your castle?"

"Well—not all of them manage to get in. Some just never make it, but I do see them out and about when I go for a walk or something."

Quinn thought about what Keaton just said, and he pictured a given number of ghosts mindlessly trying to enter the house, with only a handful finding a way inside or, perhaps, being allowed to enter. If not everyone who wished to come inside Keaton's home for whatever reason succeeded in getting in, a number of possible explanations could come into play.

There was the house's physical placement as a structure that had been built on a spot that happened to be the thinnest separation between the world of mortals and the world of the lost dead. If this were the cause of the ghosts' low success rate in breaching Keaton's sanctuary, it was likely the overlapping elements of the world of mortals somehow playing a role in neutralizing essences from the dead. In a manner of speaking, that is. Quinn imagined the heat from a well-lit fireplace keeping the incoming winter air at bay when a window in the room was left open. The analogy certainly made sense.

Of course, a second reason would be Keaton himself, being not only a living, breathing mortal, but one who also took up some real estate in a world that was never meant for him. He'd be the lit fireplace in this instance.

They paused by the second floor balustrade, with Keaton leaning against it.

Quinn took a moment to catch his breath as well, and he idly glanced at an open window at the far end of the second floor hallway as he waited. He could see nothing but the night sky and some clouds sluggishly moving against it, their tattered shapes illuminated with a dull light from the moon, wherever it might be now. And yet Quinn felt a steadily creeping terror at the sight of the window, something so primal lodged deep inside him catching on to something at the window that he couldn't see.

Yes, there was something at the window. He knew it, sensed it, though he saw nothing, and that presence was crawling inside, having just spotted him. Nothing but pure animal instinct convinced him it was there, breaching the house's questionable defenses.

"What's that?" he hissed, moving closer to Keaton and groping around for his companion's hand without tearing his gaze from the window and the thing entering it. "Do you see it?"

Keaton didn't answer at first. He'd had his head bowed for a moment as he caught his breath, but at Quinn's terrified whispering, he turned around and looked up, frowning at the window. His frown almost immediately turned to shock, then horror, then full-on panic.

"Run!" he cried, bolting up the last flight of stairs with Quinn barely managing to keep up behind him. "Hurry!"

Quinn never knew till then just how infectious abject terror could be, and it certainly didn't help that he was already close to being frightened out of his wits. Fear piled upon fear pushed him closer and closer to madness, and he'd yet to find out exactly what it was climbing through that window that had affected him in such an extreme way. Even the unflappable Keaton appeared to be just as terrified.

Wood weakened by accelerated age cracked under their heavy and frantic stomping. Quinn whimpered and tightened his grip on the balustrade when two steps literally broke under his weight, and he was barely able to save his feet just as they sank into the newly formed holes. And even as they raced up the precarious stairs for safety, Quinn could feel—too easily at that—the presence following them, incoherent and horrifying in its fury, which Quinn knew too well was directed toward him.

The encroacher. The unwanted extra body. The cause of the imbalance that surely threatened the souls aimlessly wandering about that world. Had he more time to consider it, Quinn would have tried to understand just how an extra living body in the land of ghosts could affect them—what it did to them specifically. Hopefully he'd be able to do just that once they were back in the normal world where they really belonged.

Quinn reached the top step when he felt the presence reach out for him, invisible mouth opening to let loose a distant and hollow shriek of rage. Female, Quinn thought—whatever entity was chasing them was female. And she was pissed as hell. Somehow he also believed her to be large and shapeless, her anger keeping her from moving as she normally would. Instead she now crawled, curved and formless fingers clawing away at old wood to propel her forward with unnatural speed. He truly didn't know where he got the idea from, but he was convinced of it, knew, deep down, he was terrifyingly correct in the mental image now crowding his horrified brain.

Quinn leapt through the door just as he felt a hand wrap around his left ankle, burning his skin with its awful chill, and he cried out in pain. He stumbled and pitched forward, arms flailing and barely able to keep his balance as his run turned into a pained limp. Keaton slammed the door shut, and it felt as though the specter's hand simply dissipated as though the thing's arm had been severed by the closing of the door.

Just outside the attic room, the entity hissed. Not heard, no, but like before, only sensed acutely. Quinn, collapsing on the floor as physical and emotional exhaustion set in, watched the door and hoped the creature would just give up then.

"Do you know what's out there?" he stammered, glancing at a pale and horrified Keaton. To his surprise, Keaton merely met his gaze and shook his head.

"No. I—I couldn't even see it—only feel it. And it just scared me enough to want to get us as far away from it as possible. It felt—too large. Too horrible."

Quinn took several tremulous breaths as he fought to gather his wits again, and he was dismayed at how much more difficult it was for him to manage it. He felt rather stuck in panic mode, and he'd broken the switch somehow. He tried to shift his weight when he realized his ankle was bothering him, and he hissed as he pulled his knee up in order to check his injury.

Keaton, apparently realizing Quinn's new predicament, hurried over and dropped to his knees.

"Oh, no—you're hurt!"

"That's an understatement." Quinn sucked in a loud breath when Keaton felt the ankle he'd been favoring. "I can walk. It just feels like a burn—kind of like how the others felt like when your friends came after me, but it's also worse because the skin feels numb now." At the look of horror on Keaton, Quinn hastily added, "Nothing's broken, I swear. Once we cross over again, I can get help. What about you, though? How're you doing?"

Keaton shook his head again, this time with an air of exhausted confusion. He stopped touching Quinn's foot, looking for all the world like a neophyte nurse who found himself in way over his head. The enigma that had lent him an aura of untouchableness wasn't there anymore, and Quinn felt as though he himself had just emerged from a dream. With the softening, distancing haze of a romantic mystery lifted, Keaton had emerged—heartbreakingly human.

The easy confidence was gone, and so was the charming naïveté. Uncertainty and concern now clouded his handsome features, the terror that had just assailed him now revealing its deeper influence through his uneasy glances around the room. Familiar objects and the comfortable feelings they once stirred appeared to rouse reluctance and doubt, though they remained unspoken. With the dreamy light in his eyes also giving way to sharp clarity and awareness, Keaton now looked so painfully vulnerable, and Quinn wished he weren't the catalyst to this forced awakening.

"I guess I'm all right," Keaton replied after a moment's awkward pause. "It's just—I don't feel so easy being here now."

Quinn nodded and reached out to press a hand against the side of Keaton's face. "I understand. I feel the same way, and, really, we shouldn't be here. It isn't our world, but—I'm grateful to your friends for looking after you all these years. I think they didn't have much of a choice since you were kind of put here, and I also think they didn't know any better in some way. Sort of adopted you—took you in—because you happened to be here."

Keaton's look of despair eased into surprise, and he even managed to smile a little. "Looks like you've been busy sorting out things in your head."

"I had to, I guess. I was made to cross over to this world for more than just a rescue mission."

Keaton was about to say something but froze, his attention immediately moving to the mirror standing just three or four feet away. His eyes widened, and his jaw dropped.

"Keaton? What..."

Quinn couldn't even finish what he wanted to say because warm, blinding light suddenly flooded the room, devouring everything in its wake. Quinn's hands flew up to shield his face, but even pinching his eyes shut did nothing to ease the awful effects of powerful magic being blasted into the attic room. He heard Keaton cry out, their voices matching each other in volume and pitch before the light faded, and everything turned pitch black just as a deafening rush of air filled his ears.

# Chapter 20

A cacophonous tsunami of voices flooded Quinn's already overwhelmed senses as his brain, whimpering and fetal and just about sucking its thumb in existential despair, refused to take any more drama in. Voices raised in a fuzzy mix of horror, worry, triumph, and—feline howling—threw him a lifeline that he instantly snatched, and they pulled him out of his current state of incoherent gibbering and into reality.

The reality of his world.

The explosion of blinding light (yes, *another one,* Quinn silently wailed) following the momentary respite of solid blackness had quickly eased into a much more muted glow from behind his eyelids, and shadows moved in to temper that further. Quinn blinked his eyes open, and with the return of full comprehension came the awareness of a really hard surface pressing against his back, and judging from the smell of still-to-be-washed linens and a few days' worth of used clothes in the hamper, he knew he was back in his beloved attic room.

Activity surrounded him, a whirl of endless movement among three—no, four—five?—no, three—people crammed inside his little sanctuary. He lay on the floor a good number of feet from the mirror, and he wondered how on earth he'd managed to clear that much distance in one go.

"He's awake! He's awake! Quinn! Dude! Talk to us!"

"Ouch. Motherfucker, that hurts. Hey, man. What're you doing here?"

Edwin, red-faced and deliriously happy, fell to his knees at Quinn's side and gently helped him sit up.

"What am I doing here? Helping Efrain bring you back. How're you feeling? Do you need a doctor?"

"Food, more like. Ow." Quinn groaned as he rubbed his face with both hands, the earth's dizzying movements finally stopping and keeping him from fainting all over again. Sitting up felt absolutely fabulous, and he couldn't wait to start moving around on more trusted ground. "Jesus—Efrain's here, you said?"

"Yeah. Right here," another voice spoke up, startling Quinn.

Efrain glanced over his shoulder from here he'd crouched several feet away, a wry little smile lighting up his face. From where Quinn sat, he spotted

Keaton's faded and slightly tattered Victorian costume, and it appeared as though Keaton was still unconscious. He was now being observed by Efrain Thorley and another young man, and it took Quinn a moment to realize the stranger was Efrain's boyfriend, Leander Caron. The couple spoke together in hushed tones, with Leander whipping out a phone from his jeans and calling someone in soft, hurried tones.

"He'll be okay," Efrain said, again glancing back to address Quinn and Edwin. "We just need to take him somewhere safe, and he can heal there. I didn't pick up on anything that's been changed in him—physically, anyway. I'll need more than my magic to go deeper than that."

"He's—he looks really thin," Quinn said, worry tightening his chest as his gaze dropped back to poor Keaton's lifeless form. "I think he's on his way to fading—like starving to death—when I crossed over the first time."

Seven times three. He wondered how Keaton was able to regenerate and renew at seven years of age and then at fourteen. Was he on the verge of dying each time, only to be saved by Glass-Dreams' incomprehensible magic? Was his life stretched out to as far as it could go, given the circumstances? And to what extent was Bethany an active participant in those cycles despite her being stuck in the world of mortals as a ghost with a purpose?

"Yeah. I can see that. He'll be getting a lot of help—a *lot*. My colleagues at the Institute of Arcane Studies already know about him and about Glass-Dreams. They're ready to take him in and help him recover."

Quinn exchanged worried glances with Edwin, who rested a hand on his shoulder and gave it a reassuring squeeze. "I got touched by ghosts, Efrain," he said with some hesitation. "I don't know if that means anything, but I'm sure they left me all kinds of burn marks on my arms and ankle."

Efrain nodded. After momentarily consulting with Leander, who looked at Quinn with a shy smile, Efrain got up and walked over to Quinn, who immediately shed his hoodie and nearly shrieked at the sight of red handprints up and down his arms. Efrain shushed him and focused. His eyes slid shut, and he held up his hands above the marks. A soft, pulsing globe of white light covered his hands till they disappeared, and soothing warmth rippled across Quinn's skin, following the slow movements of Efrain's magic. It only took a minute per arm, but it still left Quinn and Edwin gaping in shock at the fading marks once Efrain was done.

"Nothing serious," Efrain piped up. "Very superficial stuff that would've healed soon enough. I just sped things up for you. How're you feeling, Quinn?"

Quinn paused, considering his answer, and found himself a tad amazed at feeling—quite peppy, all things considering. He blinked and looked up at his and Keaton's rescuer. "Pretty good, actually. I seriously thought I wasn't going to make it over there. It was—everything was just too much for me, but I eventually figured it was because—obviously—I wasn't supposed to be there. Two live bodies in a world of ghost limbo and stuff? Not a good thing."

Efrain's cockeyed little smile returned, and he chuckled. "That sounds about right. You'll have to brief me on this. Oh, actually—you'll have to brief a dozen of us about this. When you're feeling better, of course. No rush. It looks like you didn't suffer some form of amnesia from the crossing over." When Quinn shook his head confidently, Efrain added, "Good. I was seriously worried I might've used too much magic to pull you two back in. Considering how long you were gone, I decided to go all in and make sure you guys were back with us in one piece."

Quinn scrunched his face. "I was out for seven hours. Was that too long?"

"Seven hours? Dude, you were out for seven days," Edwin stammered, frowning. "You didn't know that?"

"No. Days? Are you messing with me? Oh, my God. Was that what Bethany meant when she said to come back in seven?" Quinn blinked several times and then glanced at the windows. "Is that why it's sunny outside and not midnight? I—just answered my question, so don't—don't bother. My brain's starting to hurt now."

"Seven hours wouldn't have been enough time for you to re-forge that link with Keaton," Efrain replied, jerking his head in the direction of Keaton's sprawled and still unconscious form. Leander, apparently used to being ignored while his sorcerer boyfriend carried on with business, stuck to Keaton's side, checking his phone now and then, looking like everything a devoted and indulgent partner could ever be. "I'm assuming you were tossed into the mirror's world so you can draw Keaton's humanity back out. I mean—I'm assuming he was acting a little weird when you first met, right? Okay, then. Your time with him was long enough to bring him back, so to speak, and loosen Glass-Dreams' hold on him even more, so I could work with it to pull you both in."

"So—when he got his regular human mojo back—and I'm not talking about magic but, you know, normal human qualities—those dead people felt something like a double-whammy of warm-blooded people hanging around in a world they shouldn't be in and chased us out," Quinn replied, scratching his head in some confusion. "So did the disturbance we caused over there help you?"

"It was like a tag team effort," Efrain said with another chuckle, and he shrugged. "They wanted you out, we wanted you back, and it worked out pretty well. Though I admit I had to camp out here in your room for a couple of days just to make sure I was around when you and Keaton finally showed up in his room."

That globular, misshapen thing hovering behind Keaton's figure in Grandma's tapestry—that would have to be the horrifying entity that had come after them. It had forced them back into the attic room and closer to the only exit they could use, which allowed Efrain to take care of the rest.

Quinn blew out a breath and nodded. "I guess I'll know more when I meet with you and—other sorcerers and mojo badasses." He glanced at Edwin. "How's Grandma? I hope she's not freaking out too much."

"She's perfectly fine. She's downstairs with Tess, getting all fat and happy with rice cakes Tess made for her. Comfort food, you know. I think she'll be dropping hints for some *champorado* soon. Tess cooked her some, like, the day after you disappeared, and she goddamn wolfed the whole pot in one sitting, man. Mind? Blown."

Quinn laughed in relief, and he threw himself at his friend for a long, tight embrace, which Edwin tearfully returned. Efrain quickly took care of Quinn's ankle and found nothing amiss there other than the red handprint, listening to Quinn's account of how he got that one and not once appearing horrified or shocked by what he'd heard.

The terrifying entity that had chased them up the final flight of stairs sounded like a manifestation of the collective energies of Glass-Dreams, according to Efrain. Death, magic, time—all coalescing into one extremely powerful and frightening form that raged against the violation of its world. By pushing two live mortals back to where the veil was thinnest, it had helped the magic coming from Efrain pull the two unwanted and dangerous trespassers back into safety, resetting the balance of the world of the lost dead.

Like the equivalent of a supernatural burp, Quinn thought. Or even a pretty horrific hairball.

"So will that mirror be destroyed now?" Quinn asked, pointing to the offending piece of furniture. "I think I'm okay with living without a mirror in here for the rest of my natural life."

"There's no way for me to neutralize it right now, but I can have it taken away as a relic for study in the Institute of Arcane Studies," Efrain replied. "It shouldn't be a problem if you get a new mirror since it won't be attached to the house's history."

"Owowowow. Owow."

Quinn yelped in surprise at the sight of a massive gray and white cat sauntering over to him, literally materializing out of nowhere. As though knowing it had just made him nearly wet his pants, the cat sat down within reach and met his gaze steadily with a pair of the roundest copper-colored eyes he'd ever seen in a feline. Quinn immediately relaxed, and he smiled and reached out a hand in welcome.

"Owowowwwow."

The cat sauntered over to him, meowing in a humorously low and rather gravelly voice. Quinn allowed it to sit on his lap for a spell of petting and cuddling while it purred.

"That's my familiar, Oliver," Efrain said as Quinn laughed and cooed and just about melted all over the cat. "He'll take care of you while we wait for help to come for Keaton. One of Oliver's abilities is healing—not in the literal medical sense, but more emotional and mental."

Without stopping his cuddling and petting, Quinn looked up and fixed his attention on Keaton, melancholy creeping back into his heart with the onset of cold, hard reality. "Will I see Keaton again after this?" he asked, hating how small his voice sounded. How childish and needy.

"I can't guarantee anything, Quinn," Efrain replied with an apologetic smile. He gently slapped Quinn's leg. "It really depends on what we find out after examining him and running tests. I don't even know if he'll remember anything from his time over there."

"Is he the first case you've seen that's, you know, like this?"

"It is. I'm sorry if I can't be any more helpful. We're all just learning as we go, even with magic. Glass-Dreams is—unique. That's an understatement, I know.

But I've heard about a world just like that, but for the most part, everything I know about that kind of a place is pure theory. If our luck holds and Keaton's memory's intact after healing, we'll be several steps closer to really understanding what that limbo is all about without anyone else stumbling into it, literally."

Quinn swallowed and nodded, forcing a watery smile at his rescuer. "It's okay. I figured the chances are pretty slim. Just—take good care of him, okay? I don't think he has any family left."

Efrain offered him a sympathetic little smile in return and inclined his head in wordless acquiescence. Footsteps pounding up the stairs and Tess's voice calling for Efrain effectively put an end to the conversation.

Within minutes Quinn was back downstairs in Grandma's arms, being scolded and wept over and loved and promised a new cat. With, of course, a generous helping of curse words pouring out of her simultaneously.

In the meantime activity swirled around them as representatives from the Institute of Arcane Studies hurried up and down the stairs, whisking Keaton away, perhaps for good. Quinn dared not watch the proceedings as he stayed with his grandmother, opting instead to stand by a window and stare at the garden beyond while holding on to Oliver, who'd followed him downstairs and resumed his comforting magic. Quinn listened to the flurry of activity behind him—the endless mix of strange voices, the occasional and welcome exclamation or question coming from either Edwin or Tess as they did their part in helping.

"Owowoww," Oliver said, and Quinn's attention was instantly drawn to the large, hefty cat in his arms.

"Hey, buddy. You've got a pretty funny way of meowing. Did sorcerers teach you how to sound different from other cats?"

"Owwwwwowwww."

"I know. It's good to be back home."

Oliver's purring went full blast, and the cat rubbed his massive, round head repeatedly and almost aggressively against Quinn's chin, tearing reluctant giggles from him that soon gave way to bright, bubbly laughter.

# Chapter 21

"Holy shit, are we out of those voodoo dolls again?"

"Looks like we are. You haven't been bagging them with other things because you don't like the customer you happen to be helping, have you?" Quinn peered out of the barricade of unopened boxes he was in the middle of unpacking in the back of the store. "We have assholes come in sometimes. I know you've threatened bad voodoo on them or something."

"No, I haven't. Was I drunk or hungover when I did that?"

Edwin stood knee-deep among merchandise he'd been pulling off the shelves and re-pricing for clearance, and he looked just as baffled as that time when they received all those boxes of unexpected merchandise not too long ago.

"No, but that doesn't mean anything, you crazy party animal." Quinn shrugged. "Who knows? Maybe people here in Dolores totally dig them, and that's all. I know I've rung up customers buying two or even three at a time."

"Damn. People around here need a hobby."

"Yeah, but that'd mean bankruptcy for us since no one's going to want to come around anymore. It's good to have a weird population."

Edwin grumbled something and went back to his task, while Quinn ducked back down and resumed his own inventory check. He'd purposefully surrounded himself with stacks of boxes, leaving only a narrow opening through which he could escape. He needed the temporary isolation, his mood going through another down swing as memories flooded his mind yet again. The conversation, despite its humorous nature, had called back similar conversations in the past, when Quinn still lived quite blissfully ignorant of Keaton's existence.

It had been seven months and counting, he told himself glumly. Seven months with nothing but a random and widely spaced update from Efrain Thorley about Keaton's progress in the Institute of Arcane Studies, at least in the beginning. After a battery of magical tests as well as normal medical and psychological ones, he'd been deemed fit and surprisingly unscathed at least mentally and emotionally, anyway.

He was, however, also dangerously close to starving to death as Quinn had suspected, and Keaton's first couple of months hidden away in the Institute of Arcane Studies were spent in food, drink, and getting his health back on track. He'd held on all that time in Glass-Dreams, but no one was still any closer to discovering the real reason for his remarkable preservation despite the obvious lack of food and water.

Oddly enough, Keaton had also displayed an ability for clairvoyance, which everyone suspected had been caused by his years deeply immersed in the world of the lost dead. Apparently, according to Efrain, there was a superficial quality to that ability that had led them to suspect its source, as true clairvoyants were normally born with the talent. All the same, Keaton was willing to work on his, and that had been the reason for his continued residence in the hallowed halls of the institute even well after his recovery. Not once had he communicated with Quinn since his rescue, but Quinn was forgiving about that, citing the intensive testing and now training Keaton was going through. He certainly never begrudged the young man any of that, but he still couldn't help the yearning. The loneliness. The occasional fantasies of what might have been or what he'd wished for himself someday.

Quinn sighed, shaking his head. "Time to focus and stop feeling sorry for my sorry-ass self," he muttered. "At least I got myself a cute cat from all this."

And he sure did, the reminder of his new darling, a male tabby he'd baptized Milton, drawing him unerringly out of his momentary funk. He'd always wondered why his family never had a pet, considering the miracles a beloved animal could bless its owners with, but Grandma had admitted the thought was never foremost in anyone's mind all those years. Hopefully now, with Milton's rambunctious and demanding presence, the Geiger domicile would be home to adopted pets for years to come.

The shop's bell rang, and Quinn went back to work, a delighted little smile playing on his lips now that Milton just indirectly made his day much better. He heard Edwin greet the customer and then oddly engage in a hushed exchange. Not that Quinn cared; he just remembered he needed to swing by the pet store for a bag of small mice toys for Milton before he tore Grandma's new thread-related project apart.

His grandmother's never-ending paranormal tapestry had been surrendered to the Institute of Arcane Studies with her proud blessing, incidentally, when Efrain explained how it could help his peers learn more about the nature of Glass-Dreams or other similar worlds. She hadn't heard from Bethany since Quinn first crossed over into Glass-Dreams—though she'd dreamt of Bethany pleading with her that same evening to call Edwin for magical help, hence the presence of Efrain—and she'd now taken up knitting. It was a good distraction for her, and she didn't mind at all that Milton also fancied her half-dozen balls of yarn. The pair had become close despite the fact Quinn was the one who'd picked Milton and went through the adoption process and was, technically, Milton's new dad. But it was all right since Grandma wouldn't be so lonely staying all alone in the house whenever Quinn was at work.

As for Bethany, well, Quinn wished her eternal peace and rest at last. His home had fallen quiet and comfortable, almost as though the duplex had finally exorcised itself of its resident phantom. He hoped, wherever she was now, that she could still look into Keaton and watch him grow old and do great things and feel the special kind of pride a mother would feel for her child.

"Excuse me," a voice suddenly spoke up close by, and Quinn's head snapped up at the sound. "I've already asked for your boss's permission, but would you be interested in having lunch with me today?"

Quinn looked up from where he sat, cross-legged on the floor with piles of paperwork around him. Peering over the boxes and down at him was Keaton—looking fresh-faced and healthy, his hair trimmed to a neat and very flattering cut, his eyes dancing with joy as their gazes met. When Quinn failed to respond right away, a bouquet of flowers suddenly appeared as Keaton held it up and out like bait.

"I'd really like it if I could spend time with you, Quinn Geiger," Keaton said, his old world ease and confidence back but without the accompanying dream-like quality.

Quinn used the time spent gathering his paperwork and setting a neat pile aside to center himself again, his voice still failing him as he worked. But once he was back on his feet and facing Keaton, the initial shock lifted, and he could speak again. He took the bouquet from Keaton with a reverence he'd never displayed toward anything before, his wide-eyed gaze not leaving Keaton's flushed but pleased features.

"Have I ever mentioned how hot you are when you're all awkward-confident like this?" he breathed, and Keaton's smile broadened.

"No, but I'll never get tired of hearing it from you."

Quinn cleared his throat in an awkward attempt at delaying the inevitable. It certainly didn't help that his overly put-upon brain was now swimming—as usual—in a sea of questions that he simply *must* satisfy as soon as humanly possible.

"Last time I talked to Efrain, he said he and other sorcerers will be coming to study the old house—your family's old house. Any idea when they'll start?"

"I think they already have. They're kind of a nocturnal group. They go at night, which is when their magic's the most powerful, from what I understand." Keaton shrugged. "And, well, no one's going to be spying on them, at any rate. They won't be bothered by nosy bystanders."

"They work pretty quietly, I guess. I haven't been bothered by noises or weird things going on next door. Same with Grandma."

"They're experts. What can I say?"

"Have you been there yet?"

Keaton drew in a deep breath. "No, not yet. But—I want to. I'd like to see it and study it as well. But mostly to see it."

When he didn't elaborate on the matter, Quinn read between the lines and nodded. Keaton had already been told of his past—the tragedy leading to his being a "foundling" in a world of aimless souls. Perhaps in time he'd be able to open up to Quinn about his thoughts and feelings about his past, but there was no rush there. Quinn could wait, and Keaton simply needed as much time as possible to find his groove and settle down to a normal life in a world that welcomed and needed him. He'd yet to learn his purpose, to find his calling, but he was very young, and he had his life ahead of him. Bright and hopeful and overflowing with so many possibilities.

Quinn bit his lip and hesitated, then he walked out of his box fort and pulled Keaton close for a long embrace. With a surge of triumph, he felt Keaton respond in turn, his arms firm and tight around his waist, and he grinned against Keaton's shoulder.

"I'd love to have lunch with you," he murmured, hating the inevitable threat of tears stinging his eyes now and misting them over. "Have you developed a preference for a certain kind of food while you were being—well, de-loused and cleaned up and trained into being a magical superhero?"

Keaton laughed and shook his head. "I'm a little overwhelmed, to be honest with you. There are so many kinds of cuisines out there, and I think I've pretty much sampled every one of them at the institute. I'll let you lead this time."

"Okay." Quinn took a deep breath. "Uh—I'm guessing what you're being trained to be is kind of classified information or something? Can't bug you about it, can I?"

"For now, yeah, it is. I'm still in the early stages. But you'll know eventually."

Quinn pulled away slightly to stare long and hard at Keaton, his eyes flitting up and down and sideways and mapping out every beloved feature, committing Keaton's beauty to memory. Hope danced in his chest, and he reminded himself to take things slowly. Let Keaton set the pace for their re-acquaintance and, perhaps, whatever came after if Keaton wished to further their connection.

"How're you feeling?" he whispered, smiling through unshed tears. "It's been a while."

"Seven months? Not that long. At least it hasn't been seven years."

"A smartass already, eh? The things they teach you over there."

Keaton moved down to kiss him chastely, and Quinn knew Edwin was watching them go lovey-dovey all over each other—most likely sporting an annoyingly smug grin, at that. And judging from the way Keaton managed the situation with an embarrassing yet flattering myopic single-mindedness, utterly ignoring the rest of the world while he wooed Quinn without a second's hesitation, it was clear he'd yet to get over what awkward social skills he'd developed from his time in Glass-Dreams. Perhaps he never would, and the more he considered it, the more Quinn didn't mind. Suddenly finding himself the center of Keaton's world at any given moment was what romantic dreams were made of, and he wasn't one to spit in Fortune's bowl.

"I'm perfectly fine. Had a few bad dreams for the first couple of months, but they went away gradually, and the sorcerers helped. They've got magic healers over there, by the way. It's pretty cool."

Quinn smiled and pulled him back down for a longer, deeper, and more thorough kiss, ignoring the coughing and throat-clearing Edwin was now doing to break them up. Maybe his friend had his limits, after all, seeing as how he was close to out-and-out necking with Keaton in the middle of a temporarily cluttered store.

Quinn relented and pulled away, stepped back, and took Keaton's hand in his free one. The bouquet tickled his nose with its sweet fragrance, and he led the way past piles of boxes and tables packed with merchandise toward the door. He glanced at Edwin on the way out and got himself an eyeroll and a firm reminder of the time when Edwin tapped his wristwatch with some emphasis. Quinn's impromptu lunch date might be the start of something extra special with Keaton, but he was still employed and on the clock. And he owed much to Edwin, whose friendship had proven itself to be wonderful, special, and simply irreplaceable. Absolutely one of a kind and of the sort he'd always be proud of.

"Thanks, man," he said, raising his bouquet up in a salute. "Be back soon."

"And you'd better not be pregnant when you do," Edwin returned.

"We'll take it slow and be careful but no guarantees," Keaton called back just as they stepped out the door, and Quinn laughed, shaking his head. "You'll be the godfather if that happens, though. I promise."

"The things they teach you over there," Quinn said again, and Keaton glanced at him with a big, beautiful grin. "You do sassy pretty well."

"I've got to keep up with the times, you know. If I want to be with you, Mr. Geiger, I want to make sure I earned it and you don't regret a single moment of your time with me. I know I don't."

Quinn bit his lip and nodded, eyes misting up again. No, he expected he'd never regret a single thing.

Sure enough, a few years down the line, on their fifth anniversary as a couple and with Keaton—now an apprentice clairvoyant—on one knee before him and holding up a ring, Quinn saw just how accurately he'd predicted his own future.

# Don't miss out!

Visit the website below and you can sign up to receive emails whenever Hayden Thorne publishes a new book. There's no charge and no obligation.

https://books2read.com/r/B-A-LFQC-SJXT

BOOKS 2 READ

Connecting independent readers to independent writers.

# About the Author

I've lived most of my life in the San Francisco Bay Area though I wasn't born there (or, indeed, the USA). I'm married with no kids and three cats.

I started off as a writer of gay young adult fiction, specializing in contemporary fantasy, historical fantasy, and historical genres. My books ranged from a superhero fantasy series to reworked and original folktales to Victorian ghost fiction.

I've since expanded to gay New Adult fiction, which reflects similar themes as my YA books and varies considerably in terms of romantic and sexual content.

While I've published with a small press in the past, I now self-publish my books. Please visit my site for exclusive sales and publishing updates.

Read more at https://haydenthorne.com.